TALLEY GULF TREASURE

ANDREA HOPE

ISBNs
Paperback: 979-8-9939175-0-4
Hardcover: 979-8-9939175-1-1
ebook: 979-8-9939175-2-8

Editor: Sherlyn Garcia
Line Editor: Carol L. Crymble
Cover Art: Tony Midi
Consultant & Formatting: Allison Buehner

For Paige, Zoe, and Ezra.

CHAPTER 1

You have opened this book into the middle of a modern-day pirate story, and I have a question for you...

"Do you hear them marching?" August mustered the courage to ask his older sister, Avril, as he followed her toward one of the buffet lines on the cruise ship. There were other restaurants on board, but this one had a view of the water. It was a perfect day to be in the middle of the ocean. There was a calm sea below and sunshine in the sky. However, August Bridges stood with his back to the view, as he pleaded with his sister to listen to him.

He could feel the worry radiating from his face, but he did not want to make a scene and draw any unnecessary attention to himself. His sister reluctantly whispered back to him with slight concern, "Who?"

"The pirates..." He nervously trailed off, shoving his hands into the pockets of his green hoodie. August was dressed for an adventure with his hoodie, cargo pants, and t-shirt. He did not care much about what he wore, as long as he was comfortable. He was stylish in an effortless way, due to his dark wavy hair and hollow cheeks that resembled his sister's. He felt silly mentioning the pirates to her, but he knew he was doing the right thing by warning her about the dangers that were lurking all around them.

Before August had a chance to continue, he saw his sister's expression curl into a mocking grin as she shoved him away. The thought of pirates existing in modern-day was ridiculous, especially on a cruise. "I thought you were going to say something useful," she decidedly taunted him, as she gathered more food on her plate using silver tongs.

Avril, who was two years older than her brother, had been forced to go on vacation with her family the summer before starting college. The only reason that she tolerated being there, was because August wanted her there and it was for his birthday. Avril had brown hair cut to her shoulders and preferred grunge clothing from the nineties rather than trends that would come and go.

August watched his sister put some extra pieces of bacon on the side of her plate for him. Avril was more of a parental figure for August than their own parents were. Their parents kept their distance from their son, and occasionally attempted to be closer with their eldest child Avril. The contrast felt to August as if they did not want to get attached to him because one day he would be gone. In the back of his mind he knew somehow, he was meant to be somewhere else.

The uneasiness of the truth boiled up in August's mind as he recalled the events from the last few days that had led them here. August found it unusual that when he asked his parents if he could go on vacation ahead of his eighteenth birthday, they agreed. He was not aware that his parents were planning to visit *old friends*. August thought the trip was his gift, but his parents turned it into a family vacation instead.

When the cruise was making its next stop on one of its mainland destinations, the Bridges family made their way to a nearby island that was not part of the ship's official route. They were exploring the markets together on their way to meet with their parent's friends that August and Avril did not know anything about prior to this trip. Avril was walking with their mom as their father led the way. August trailed behind his family.

Whispering voices sounded around August as he walked, which caused him to look up from his shoes. He saw a woman looking right at him, pointing, and whispering to another person. He could not understand what the strangers were saying, but he knew they were talking about him. Their expressions were haunted by fear. Their anxiety was not directed at the rest of his family, but was only directed toward him.

Unusual looking guards with thick, leather coats then approached the Bridges family. They seemed well spoken and serious. Discreetly, the guards recommended that August leave the island. To August's surprise, his parents defended him being there, but the guards continued to ask for him to leave to due to the upheaval that his presence caused. His parents looked at each other with knowing glances, as if to express that they should have been more careful. As his parents stepped away with the guards to discuss the disturbance, August tried to eavesdrop, all he could hear were the words '*grace, page,* and *August.*' He was baffled when his parents quickly changed their minds about wanting him to be there, and they encouraged their son to leave with the guards. August would have protested, but he saw the stringent look on his father's face. August wondered if he was in danger as he noted the sympathetic look his sister gave him before he was taken back to the ship.

August attempted to calm himself down after having to return a few hours before his family. He began wandering around the ship mindlessly; for him, nothing good ever came from doing anything mindlessly.

Tracing his fingers along the hallway walls, he passed by a room that had an open door. August heard a splash. He turned back with curiosity to see what caused the noise. His dark turquoise eyes widened, as he looked through the open door. An old wooden plank was hanging over the edge of a modern balcony. A frigid chill surged through his body and his face was filled with terror as he was discovered. Stark, cold eyes were looking back it him from a man with bands that were tied all the way up his sleeves on both arms, and who wore a small silver skull and cross-bones broach with a chain. This was the pirate captain. August tried to run, but he was caught. He was tied up in ratty nets, but the low quality of the nets allowed for his quick escape.

August's heart was beating as hard as it could, as he leaned against one of the walls to catch his breath. That is when he heard the marching for the first time. Everything seemed to slow down, as he sluggishly moved his head to the right. It felt like being in a dream where someone was chasing him and he could only move in slow motion, yet this was real. He saw the pirates chasing after him, but their movements sounded like marching. The more August learned, the more he realized they were not just modern-day pirates; they were their own breed, a seemingly unfortunate mystical lot. Their marching was like a curse on their prey. August could not escape the disorientation the marching caused. His enemies tied him up once more, only this time upside-down to disorient him further. They watched him closely until they fell asleep.

August wished his father would have allowed him to buy the swords, daggers, and other weapons at the shop they had visited in the market on the island before boarding. His father always told him; there would be time for weapons when he was older. That notion did not help him in his current predicament, nor did he understand what his father meant. He was already seventeen years old. August thought that if he had a weapon, he could have saved the person that must have been forced off the plank. His hope was that somehow the anonymous person had survived. It was only a blur he had seen out of the corner of his eye before he heard the splash. He tightened his eyes shut in agony. Why did he have to hear the splash of a person hitting the water? Why did he have to catch a glimpse? August felt selfish for praying it was not someone he knew or loved.

Whilst the pirates rested, August used the ridge of a coin to saw at the net. Shortly after, the rope snapped. Since he was used to playing upside-down on the playground back home when he was younger, August landed on his feet. Once the pirates realized he escaped, they continued to chase him all over the ship. Many of them were in disguise as passengers and ordinary cruise line workers. This was their way of luring more passengers onto the ship to add to their growing numbers. They were building a small army of mutineers. August did not know what to do, but he knew who he had to warn. He quickly and quietly made his way back to his sister.

The distance of the marching was less disorienting now as he stood in the buffet line with Avril, than it had been when he was in the same hallway as the noise. He deduced that he had a little bit more time to protect his sister. August was more concerned with warning Avril about what he witnessed than warning his parents. He would not even know where to look for them since they were not in their room. He did know where to find Avril though, as she preferred the pool and the buffet.

"I'm serious," August insisted, pushing closer to his sister after having found her. He sounded rattled and jittery, which he could tell caught her off guard. "In the back of the ship," he stated with a quiet plea, "I saw a real plank!"

Avril squinted her eyes in response to what her brother said. She did not seem to believe him, yet surprisingly replied, "Well, if that's what you saw, I guess that means you can show me then." Avril smiled at him, and he followed her over to a table with comfortable seating, so at least she could have her meal first. She was not being unkind to her brother, despite her skepticism and teasing nature, but August knew she was not taking him seriously.

Instead of sitting in the chair next to Avril, August kneeled beside her gripping the arm of the chair with frustration, holding back his volume, he intensely communicated, "No! Did you not hear me? They're marching!"

Avril deeply sighed. August could tell that she was trying to help him, but she did not understand that it was a real problem. "Marching? What is that supposed to mean?" She asked him before taking another bite of fruit from her plate.

From August's experience, the sound of marching meant the pirates were in pursuit. It was chilling to hear the marching pause, while knowing the enemy was so close. "I have to hide. Don't follow me. Find mom and dad! Stay with them. I'll come and find you later." August insisted in a serious but hushed voice as his eyeline led to a nearby cabinet, leaving his sister to choose her own fate.

He swiftly ran and opened the bottom doors of one of the white floor-to-ceiling cupboards that were built into a row in the wall of the restaurant. August expected that he would need to move dishes or other supplies to hide, but the space was already empty. He ducked inside and closed the door behind him, turning himself around in the space to have his face toward the exit so he could listen.

August did not know that only people who knew about the pirates could hear their impending steps, or he would never have warned his sister Avril.

Avril set her fork down as she turned her head slightly. She, too, could now hear the marching. Once Avril had the auditory evidence, she stood up calmly as to not bring about any notice to herself. Despite August's instruction, Avril followed her brother's lead by crawling into an adjoining cabinet.

The marching suddenly stopped.

Avril was thinking that this must be the worst practical joke that had ever been played on her, and by worst she meant scariest. She was getting annoyed, and slightly popped open the cabinet door with her foot to move August's perceived game along.

"He must have gone in here!" One of the pirates shouted. Avril giggled as if giving them another clue to their location.

She could not hold this prank against her brother, as she was the one who was always making jokes, inventing games, and causing mischief for the two of them. It was her way of making sure her brother was not alone, and that her family stayed together. However, this was her vacation, too, and she wanted to spend it relaxing and mentally preparing for college. Pranks and games were not part of her plan. It was bad enough that she wasted time on the island with her parents when they did not even end up finding their parent's friends. It would be better if this game ended sooner rather than later so she could finish her breakfast and get back to the pool.

However, the marching sound was scary, and since when did her brother have friends? It reminded her of a nightmare she had when she was little before her family had moved. Avril had almost forgotten that they had lived somewhere else before the house she and her brother grew up in.

Now, those who were marching were in the very same room with them. Avril stopped making noise and pulled her foot back into the cabinet. What if it was not a game?

"He is in here," a voice said. August held his breath.

August was fighting with his fear, knowing he could not make a sound. The pirates would find his sister because she was the source of the noise, and they would make her walk the plank. To save his sister later, he had to be silent now. August held his breath, being as brave as he could muster, while Avril was taken away. The memory of her screams would ring in August's ears forever.

He remained sitting in the cabinet silently when he heard the pirate captain's footsteps approaching. It was a more distinct sound, as the boots were heavier than the others on the wooden floor. The sound stopped right in front of where August was hiding. Then, surprisingly, the pirate captain turned around and left. This puzzled August for a moment. However, the faux captain's strategy became clear to August. The enemy was using August's sister as bait to lure him out of hiding. To August, this was a clear challenge to act. This challenge would end in his sister's rescue or his own capture.

The pirates needed everyone who knew they existed to disappear and disappearance was the pirate captain's specialty. If anyone saw any of their suspicious dealings, their fate would be sealed. August could not allow this to take place. He wondered how deep the infiltration ran. The pirate captain and the real captain could be one in the same person, but August did not know. He needed to think strategically not only to keep himself safe, but he needed to save his sister and potentially everyone on board the ship. August wanted to be a hero and thought about fighting back, but he knew he was not strong enough on his own. He remained still; he did not know what to do.

Suddenly, August fell backwards through the thin, white, wall of the cabinet behind him. He was now in a pitch-black room adjacent to the restaurant. August's heartbeat was loudly pumping in his ears and he could no longer control his breathing. He struggled to his feet and then stood completely still in a hunched posture with his arms out ready to defend himself. He hoped the pirates outside did not hear, but was uncertain of who or what remained in the dark around him.

A light snapped on revealing a man who looked like he should be the real captain due to his commanding presence. He was standing in front of August with a wide grin on his face, as if he was expecting the intruder. "Hello, August, we've been waiting for you."

August's focus honed in on the opening that he fell through that was now being sealed. He tried to make a run for it before it was too late to escape, but the man took hold of August's collar. "No need for that. We aren't going to hurt you. My name is Captain Hank, and I am the *real* captain of this ship. The pirates took over a few months ago. So far, I have managed to save these people behind me from the plank. I saved the latest one today." It was the same person August witnessed being forced off the plank earlier. Even though he barely saw it happen, the memory was clearer to him after he saw the face of the survivor. The captain continued speaking, "We haven't secured the ship yet, but the pirates haven't been able to find us in here." He hunched down to August's eye level, "I'm glad you're here though, kid. Now, let's figure out how to save your sister."

Captain Hank's presence radiated trust. However, August's peace only lasted for a moment, as the next words out of the captain's mouth would change August's life. "This may sound strange, but I had a dream that a boy named August was going to be important to our survival. You are August, aren't you?" Captain Hank confirmed with slight suspicion in a lowered voice.

"Yes, but I..." August attempted to interject, but was cut off by Captain Hank who was presumably too excited about his dream giving him foresight.

"In my dream you were hesitant to help us, but the passengers and I have everything you could possibly need right here. Even pieces for the walls – like the one you fell through. Vana and James have already fixed it, so the pirates will be none the wiser if they were to check those cabinets for you."

August did not want to interrupt the man, so he waited until he could speak again. He spoke quickly as he did not know how long of a pause the captain would take, "Yeah, well

– that's great and all, but I don't actually know how to help. I don't know what to do – I'm not an adult. I'm only seventeen!"

Captain Hank stared at the kid for a moment. "I was sailing boats by myself at twelve." August was baffled by the concept. They exchanged judgmental glances. The adult continued, "Kid, I dreamt - that you could help turn the tide on our situation. You are here to save us, and we are going to help you do it. I figured you would be an asset to our side. You were going to attempt a rescue anyway, were you not? So, you might as well accept our help to save your sister. She might be saved if you act, but if you act alone, she may not be saved at all. If it was not for us, you would have been found eventually, and given your significance you would be killed. We have the wisdom, equipment, weapons..."

"Weapons?" August asked in confirmation. It was the magic word he needed to hear to take the captain seriously. "Only for my sister's sake, I'll join you." Before the mention of weapons, August was overwhelmed especially after hearing that he was thought of as significant. This must have been why he was made to leave the island. The pirates and the islanders must have thought that he was someone important. They must have mixed him up with another August. With the mention of weapons and the promise of saving his sister, August was on board with helping the captain and his passengers.

"Good decision. You'll be safer with us, too." Captain Hank led August further into the secret room. There were boxes and supplies scattered everywhere. As the captain had stated, they had a little bit of everything in preparation against the opposition they were facing. There was barely any room to walk.

Captain Hank gave August a tour of the hidden, storage room that he called the *hideout*. The space was a very large room that the passengers had crafted into a survival base. It was cluttered with supply crates with different areas between the walls of boxes. Captain Hank showed August around the cluttered corners and different pathways of their dining area, bathrooms, and triage space. He said, "August, if you feel like resting for a bit, you can do so over there." He pointed to some makeshift bunks, and continued, "You can join me in our strategy area, which is next to the dining area, when you are ready to get to work." The captain's statement was considerate, as August was exhausted from the last twenty-four hours. Even though it was day now, he could not tell in the hideout.

August sauntered over to the side of the room the captain had pointed to, and sat with the others his age. He continued to observe in silence. The others were whispering about him, as the islanders had done. August was emotionally and physically drained. There was a heaviness in his heart and a weight on his shoulders that he had not experienced before. The thought crossed his mind that nothing good or positive was left in his life aside from the prospect of food, weapons, and a bathroom. This was something August had been subconsciously praying for since his last entrapment by the pirates. What else does a person need in life? Yet, he wanted to escape his newfound obligations.

August got back up and walked a few feet towards one of the rows of crates.

"Oh! Pardon me," said a young, English girl apologetically. She had tripped over August's feet amidst all the clutter. "I didn't see you over the boxes. You're new, are you not?"

August's eyes widened when he saw the girl in front of him. Everything slowed down for him like it had when he heard the marching, only this time there was no marching it was the radiance of a beautiful girl. He nervously answered her question as quickly as possible like he had been startled awake in class and forced to answer a homework question, "Yes, I'm new. I'm here because the pirates have taken my sister, Avril."

The girl's eyes widened in response, and she lunged toward him. "Shh!" The girl said pulling August beneath the boxes, underneath a partly covered table, away from prying eyes and listening ears. She covered his mouth with her hand, and whispered in a serious tone, "Don't you know what happens to those who are taken at this time of day?" After the initial shock of being yanked down to the floor by someone he did not know, a chill ran through his body. An unknown threat lingered in the silence between her words. The girl continued to inform him, "Those the pirates take - have the option to join the pirates to become one of them. They can choose that life or they must walk the plank."

Her eyes shone with sincerity and knowledge. Unlike the captain, this girl made him feel safe. With her it was as if the world was not on his shoulders, she shared the weight with him. His impression of her was that she knew enough for the two of them. If he failed, she would not. This empowered August.

He wanted to ask her name, but she was still educating him, while creating a solid first impression. "They are not real pirates. Most of them are wannabees who don't know anything that real pirates do. They are made up of stolen civilians, and the leaders are too selfish to realize how infiltrated their crew has become. Only a handful of passengers have walked the plank, and those who do - we try to rescue. It's all gotten rather out of hand." The girl finally took a deep breath. Her exasperation radiated as she seemed lost in thought for a moment.

August quipped sarcastically to her, "It sounds like they have it down to me."

Unintentionally, she let out a slight laugh at his unexpected joke. August realized it was a bit strange to use humor when he just lost his sister to piracy. It was something Avril would have done, make jokes in a trying moment. He shared his sister's sense of humor, but it was not as much of a coping mechanism for him as it was for Avril. He smiled briefly, knowing what he said was not funny, but his comedic use of sarcasm was amusing to this stranger as well as to himself. In a manner that was more his own, he nervously added, "So is my sister safe?"

"As long as she chooses to keep her life and join the pirates." The girl answered as she fixed her shoe laces.

August guessed, "I think she would."

The girl looked right into his eyes, "All the same, we better make sure of it."

The intensity made him flinch. He asked her, "How?"

"That's why I dragged you under here. I know where they keep their captives, but we don't want the others to hear us. Let's go see your sister." The blonde girl gestured to the table they were under, and answered with bright eyes and a very adventurous, resourceful smile. As she spoke, she pulled up part of the wooden floor beneath them which revealed a secret wooden staircase. With no resistance or hesitation, the girl dropped down into the mysterious small space and began to descend the stairs.

August noticed a table filled with flashlights nearby, so he quickly grabbed two of them and followed his new ally into the unknown.

CHAPTER 2

August quietly followed the girl who seemed to have all the answers to his questions. She was a breath of fresh air to him in contrast to all the stuffy adults and solemn looking children they had left behind in the hideout. August felt like he was escaping the pressure of Captain Hank's supposed foresight, while still accessing achievement in his plans to rescue his sister.

"This is kind of cool." August assumed he had said these words to himself, and not out loud the way that he did.

However, the girl beside him asked, "You said this was cool? Did you not?" For a fleeting moment, August thought she could read his mind. He had spoken quietly, but she was in proximity to August. "I think so, too," she said after he did not reply.

Her pace paused for a moment, but August had not noticed and kept moving, almost knocking her down. She took a deep breath, holding her finger to her lips, in a gesture of silence.

"Sorry," he whispered, instantly regretting his choice to utter a sound. August could hear the reasoning for the sudden halt in her steps. The pirates were marching again. The girl slapped her hand over August's mouth once more, pulling him back into a small, dark corner and turning off their flashlights.

Her plan of silence was interrupted by an onset of hiccups. "Quick, give me your jacket!" She quietly insisted. He obliged, handing it over to her rapidly, as she muffled the sounds. August had his arms around her, and she buried her face into his sleeve to muffle the sounds further.

August heard the pirate captain's voice in the distance. The same chill surged through his body as it had the very first time. "The boy's sister must be made to join us in our quest, but the boy must never step foot on the island. If you find him again – kill him." At this point, August was not surprised by the demand. This must have been the reason the guards wanted him to leave the island. He was being mistaken for someone who was important.

August wondered how long the pirates had control of the ship, since he and his family had been on this voyage for almost a week. The pirates must have been stealing people from every batch of newly boarded passengers. August assumed the girl in his arms had been dodging the pirates for quite some time, as she knew of the secret staircases and corridors. He was grateful for her, but he also wanted to know more about the knowledge she possessed. She seemed to have an understanding about what they were up against.

Time felt as though hours had passed by, as they sat in the dark and silence. They had no way of knowing it had only been twenty minutes. August was creating a list of things he wanted to ask this new girl he had befriended. He also wondered what Captain Hank's plan for him was going to be, as he had not gotten a chance to ask before jumping into action. A twinge of guilt crept into August's mind for leaving the others behind because he did not know when, or if, he would return. However, August had every intention of saving everyone if he could. He did want to be a hero and a leader, yet he was following a girl whose name he did not even know.

August longed to stretch his arms and legs, as he was beginning to lose feeling in his limbs. He also did not prefer the dark, but he was too old to let others know about his fear. When the light was turned back on without warning, he was frightened by it. August was not expecting it, and thought the pirates had found them. His new ally gave him a look of amusement at his fearful reaction. He blushed.

The girl grinned and with a upbeat tone she spoke, "Did you hear the way they were marching? Marching has two meanings. One meaning is that they are in pursuit, but the other is that they have a new pirate in their group." Both teens stretched out their legs to allow the return of blood flow. With the light, and freedom to move, August could focus on the task at hand without his mind wandering in discomfort.

"So, is my sister a pirate?" August questioned.

"What? No. They are in pursuit right now. The marching pattern is different. Didn't you hear it?" The girl answered him. He seemed dumbfounded by her knowledge. He could tell that she was realizing for the first time that he was not only new to their group, but that he was newly boarded.

Instead of giving him back his jacket, she put it on while telling him, "The pirates are looking for us in the wrong place. Even if they do offer your sister an option of becoming one of them, they won't find us now. We can focus on rescuing her." She pointed up to steps that led to a small window. "There you should be able to see the prisoners. The ones who agree to be pirates will live past midnight, and those who do not will potentially die at noon. Your sister should be there."

August responded quietly, "I spent the last sunrise tied upside-down in a net. I don't wish that on anyone else." He looked out of the small window, and he saw a modern cruise ship balcony, like the one he had spotted when he first discovered the pirates. Only this time, there was no old, wooden plank. The more August thought about it, the more he began to believe the pirates used a plank ritualistically and not as an act of convenience. Similarly, to the bands they wore on their arms, it could not have been comfortable. The pirates seemed to have rules that aligned with an unknown mythology and not traditional piracy.

August looked back to the girl, and spoke a little louder down to her, "Avril is the only one on the balcony. No pirates or other prisoners."

He slid open the tiny window, "Psst – Avril."

Avril answered, in a twisted agony, "August?"

Her brother continued, "Listen, don't walk the plank. You have to become a pirate at midnight or you won't live to see another day. They will make you walk the plank at noon if you don't join them."

The English girl stepped up beside August and added emphasis to further prove the point. "Avril, I know you don't know me, but accept being a pirate. Listen to what your brother is telling you to do. I have seen it happen. It's your best chance to survive this. Your brother and I will come to save you."

She then turned her attention to August, seemingly changing her mind on what their current plan was going to entail. "Does your sister know how to use a knife?"

August shrugged his shoulders. "I guess."

The girl successfully reached her arm as far she could through the window. Avril's hands were not tied, so she reached as far as she could through the net. Once Avril cut herself free, she realized that despite her slender frame she could not escape through the window. The circle was too small. If she tried to leave through the doors, the pirates would be on the other side.

"What do I do?" She whispered in exasperation as she looked around.

The English girl rapidly answered the question. "Don't worry about coming back with us now, it's okay. We just needed you out of the net. Tell the pirates you are already one of them. Tell them that you are truly disgusted with the way they let you escape – that it was a test and they have failed it. Tell them to wait for the captain's orders."

August looked out of the corner of his eye, as the girl spoke about the captain. They both knew from the conversation they overheard from the leader of the pirates, that he intended on Avril becoming one of them. The passengers had Captain Hank, whereas the pirates had their own captain. Avril would have to act as if the pirate captain was the real captain, but they knew that he was not the true captain of the ship.

The girl continued, "They will have to get the pirate captain. If somehow you can defeat the captain in an altercation – the ship is yours. You would be the new captain - according to their rules. However, you'll have better odds if you just focus on convincing them you're a pirate. Try to escape, but just focus on your safety. If you must become a pirate, we will do our best to save you before it happens."

"Be brave," August stated with a nervous smile through the window, as the girl dragged him away. If something worse happened to his sister, he did not want the last thing she saw of him to be fear. He wanted her to see his smile.

The blonde girl was looking at her shoes as she walked, and she softly said to August, "That wasn't my original plan, but she seemed capable. She'll easily trick the pirates into thinking she's a legitimate pirate, unless their captain gets involved."

August looked over at her, "It's a good plan..."

"...But?" She heard the uncertainty of his statement.

"I'm worried she won't be able to do it," August admitted. It was obvious that Avril would have to do her best to trick the pirates if she wanted to live. The two teenagers were quiet. They were right outside the hidden room. The girl led August back through a different corridor in case they were followed. There was an edge of light around the doorway. The light illuminated the sides of their faces.

The girl took a deep breath. "Back there - I heard Avril call you August. Are you - *the August* - who Captain Hank is convinced we cannot win back the ship without?"

"Oh, so you heard about that?" August bashfully chuckled. His eyes widened as he turned his face toward hers and with a humble cadence said, "I have the same name as the guy your captain keeps dreaming about – it's no big deal. I'm no dream come true," he joked.

The girl stoically responded, "Well, Captain Hank's dream did come true. That is how he knows so much about what is going on. You probably do not want to hear about that right now, while you are coming to terms with being 'the savior' and all." She joked, while still holding something back.

The girl knew Captain Hank was the only one on the ship who could dream. No one else had been able to dream since their voyage began. She learned a lot of information the good captain would have deemed too dangerous for her to know. That did not stop her from scurrying throughout the labyrinths of passageways within the ship that she frequently traveled. The real captain would have put a stop to it if he had known. She would sneak into places even he would not dare to enter, including where the two teens had spoken with Avril.

"People having dreams about me? Yeah. That's not creepy at all," August quipped about him being the focus of the prophetic dreams. He could tell they were both attempting to deescalate their stress with lighthearted banter.

"It's not all about you," she snickered, bumping into him. "You have nothing to do with the secret corridors and the resource loots that the captain dreams about." She exaggerated playfully, recognizing that this was the first friend she had in a long time. The blonde girl introduced herself, "My name is Helena."

He reached out his hand to shake hers, "I'm August Bridges." As Helena shook his hand with a bright smirk, August realized he was also smiling back at her with just as much delight. He knew he was in trouble. He already liked this girl.

CHAPTER 3

Meanwhile, Avril was left alone, stuck in enemy territory. The net she was trapped in was now on the floor; thanks to the knife she retrieved from August's new friend. Avril kicked the netting with her foot. She could hear voices coming from the other side of the door from where she stood on the balcony. It was a nice sized space, and under different circumstances the balcony would have been very peaceful. The sounds of muffled conversation were a chilling contrast to the calm, soothing, sound of the sea. Avril focused on her breathing. The only way she was going to convince anyone that she was a pirate, was if she remained calm. She touched the wall to steady herself as the voices grew closer. Avril placed the knife in her front pocket, crossed her arms, and lifted her face to the sky to get into the persona of being a pirate.

One of the pirates walked through the door to see Avril standing free of the net. He was not the pirate captain, but he did seem competent and important. He was carrying weapons that were more impressive than the knife she had secured. He had blonde hair, blue eyes, and a couple bands on his arms. Avril could see the edge of a tattoo peeking out from under one of his arm bands. He looked more like a pirate then the others she had seen.

Brazenly, Avril asked him, "Do you know who I am?"

Though the pirate was taken back by her attitude he answered, "Yes. I do."

This was not the response Avril was hoping for. She raised an eyebrow, following his quick retort with another question, "Tell me then, who am I?"

The pirate smiled, answering, "Not a pirate."

Avril's expression fell, but her confident tone did not waver as she asked, "What happens to me if you're right, and I'm not a pirate?" She already knew the answer, but she wanted to see if she could learn anything else. Avril fully believed that her brother and his friend would come to her rescue, and it allowed her to act with more confidence.

"Typically, you would walk the plank. It's an old fashion tradition, but effective. If you choose to keep your life and become a pirate, but then decide you don't want to follow orders – we have this." The pirate showed her a vial, and inside the vial was a clear liquid. "A gift from the captain. It takes away human senses. I promise it hurts more than it sounds." Sounding more intimidating than he looked, he put the vial back into a pocket in his leather vest. He continued, "Follow me."

Avril followed the steps of the pirate. Avril took a deep breath as she noticed they were about to enter a conference room with other pirates. She had remained calm so far, but she could feel her teeth begin to chatter, so she clenched her jaw and clasped her hands together tightly to stay in control.

There did not seem to be any other captives, just her. The pirate she was with stopped before entering the door. Without looking at her face he asked. "Do you see the door at the end of the hall to your right?"

"Yes," she answered.

In a gruff whisper, he instructed, "That door leads to the buffet you were taken from, where your brother disappeared. In five seconds, you are going to run and I am going to chase you. Make it look real... *run!*" Avril fled.

I n another part of the ship, August was feeling as if a whole new world was beginning in the most intriguing way possible.

He once again followed Helena, as she opened the door beside them and they walked back into the light of the hideout. As they made their way inside, the brilliance of the emergency and fairy lights used in the hideout made them blink, and Helena put away their flashlights.

"Have you noticed how loud the marching gets?" She asked August as they moved through the crowded room of boxes, but continued speaking, "There must be a lot of pirates on this ship now. I guess people would rather be pirates then be killed by them."

August scrunched his face, struggling for the right words. He asked her, "With all the fake pirates involved, are we truly at risk? Even the people that walk the plank are saved. Has anyone been in real, mortal danger?"

Helena stopped in her tracks, gesturing for August to look at one of the adults. August and Helena were well protected behind the stacks of materials in storage, but they could still see the individual from around the bend. The man they were observing was a person that August had seen earlier in the day. This man was sitting at a table talking to Captain Hank.

Helena pointed. "He did die. He was once a real pirate, not like those other phonies that get scared into it. Only, in his culture you must confront your leader if a doubt is spoken. It is kind of interesting, don't you think?"

She looked up at August watching the thoughts dance across his face.

Helena could tell that August was seeing their predicament in another light. He looked down at her, noticing her gaze, and the corner of his mouth turned up into a smile. Helena stared back for a moment, but then rolled her eyes in lighthearted amusement. She continued, moving through the riddled mess, and August followed her.

"If that guy is doubting. What is he doubting?" August asked.

This thought seemed to merit more of an immediate reaction from Helena. A puzzled expression took over her face like the pirates took over the ship. Helena answered his question, "My best guess is that he doubts you would be able to save everyone, or worse - he might have doubt in my dad."

"Your dad?" August questioned in return.

Helena replied nonchalantly, "Yes, my dad, the real captain of the ship, Captain Hank."

CHAPTER 4

That night as everyone slept, August remained awake as the clock ticked closer to midnight. He could not rest knowing that his sister may not be okay. August was concerned about their parents, as well, he needed to know if they were in danger. August wondered if they had attempted to alert the cruise line's staff of his and Avril's disappearances. He pondered if they, too, had been caught.

Thoughts of the strange happenings on the island returned to August. First, they had kicked him off the island, then the pirates wanted him dead, and then he learned that Captain Hank had prophetic dreams about him. What was it about him that had caused such a disturbance? Why did he want to go on this vacation in the first place? August felt as if he brought this situation upon himself by wanting to be somewhere else for his birthday. He revisited the thought that he had to save everyone. He believed he was going to die in the process, whether he died a hero or not, was yet to be determined. He tossed and turned as he mulled over the events, but his mind then turned to Helena.

August sat up, then went with determination to try to find the secret stairs that Helena had shown him during the day. Those stairs would potentially lead him back to Avril if he could find the way. He bumped into a wall or two as he searched around. The atmosphere in the crowded space was spookier at night, with the supply boxes everywhere. August could not find his flashlight; he must have misplaced it earlier when he was having dinner with Helena. His palms began to sweat. He was already lost and confused in this space which led him to feel a bit panicked. His heart began racing, the way it had when he was being chased the day before. Feeling lost, he felt for the pockets of his jacket but his jacket was gone, too. His breath grew shallower as he was having a panic attack.

A hand took hold of August's shoulder; he shot around letting out an alarmed shout. He shook as he tried to catch his breath. As lights were being turned on, others in the room were asking each other what was happening.

"August, what are you doing?" asked the kind Captain Hank. August had not seen the man since Helena revealed him to be her father. He seemed much too old to be Helena's dad, but August had no reason to doubt her on such a matter.

Where was Helena anyway? She was probably scurrying about the ship doing the incredible, hero acts that he should be doing himself. Instead, he was standing here unintentionally making a scene. Worse than that, he could not even answer the man coherently due to being lightheaded from his panic attack. August muttered before collapsing. August's back hit the floor, but Captain Hank kept the boy from hitting his head.

Captain Hank, continuously more unimpressed with August, looked up to see his daughter Helena through the crowd of people. She looked concerned as if she already knew who the fainter was.

"It's a good thing this room is soundproof," Helena commented as she sauntered over to her father. She seemed to be trying not to alarm him. However, the speed in her approach would not have surprised him regardless as much as her presence did in general. Captain Hank thought that Helena had been killed two months prior.

The crowd had not yet dissipated around them, yet Helena kept eye contact with her father. As Captain Hank placed August down on the ground, Helena slid in next to him. "August?" she whispered to the boy.

Captain Hank spoke his daughter's name in a painfully guttural, low voice, "Helena?" The boy did not respond to his name being called, neither did the girl to hers. Captain Hank questioned louder, to be sure, he was not going mad by seeing her, "Helena?"

"What?" She questioned sharply, standing to face him.

He swallowed nervously, "You – are you – a – a..."

"... a ghost?" she haughtily finished his sentence, with a smile and an eager look in her eyes. She answered, "No, sir."

"Are you alive?" Captain Hank inquired further, not quite believing his eyes. August unintentionally interrupted the strained reunion with a cough.

"Dad, August could probably use some water," she suggested to her father.

"Water!" The captain called out sharply, and someone quickly supplied a bottle to him. The captain watched as Helena gently splashed a bit of water on August's face. She playfully splashed some of the water back at her father as well. He could see that Helena still harbored the same spirit of fun as she once did and it gave him some peace of mind that it was truly his daughter. Helena aided August in drinking the rest of the water.

"What were you doing, August?" Captain Hank asked August carefully as the disoriented teen woke up.

August answered, "I was gonna go find my family."

"Oh," the captain said to himself, as if the thought had never occurred to him before.

The rest of the interlopers in the room were all going back to sleep, so Captain Hank and Helena picked August up off the floor and brought him over to their medical triage area. This space was quite small, which Captain Hank knew annoyed his daughter greatly.

"How were you going to find your family?" Captain Hank scolded August, after a long delay. He, much like his daughter Helena, let August's words sink into his thoughts before responding. August did not have a good answer, so he simply shook his head in defeat at the question. Captain Hank was still reeling with frustration from finding out his daughter was still alive and that she did not return sooner to tell him. He redirected his pain and anger to August instead of communicating his feelings to his daughter, "I said you would save us all, not kill us all! It's a good thing I discovered you. You almost got yourself killed with that fall, and you didn't even leave the room!" The man was nearly shouting, probably keeping some of his people from their sleep.

August appeared to be fighting the tears welling up in his eyes. Helena noticing the embarrassment and anger showcased on his face, stated, "Dad, stop yelling at him," she snapped back at the fuming captain. Captain Hank looked back into Helena's stubborn eyes and mellow face. He handed the girl a towel to place on August's forehead. When Helena thought that August had fallen asleep, she spoke to her father. "I managed to escape the pirates. Death nor piracy seemed like a good option to me."

"You've been gone for two months, Helena!" Captain Hank stated.

"Well, I never said that I didn't die. I did die, I think..." Helena trailed off. Shock and disbelief turned the captain's face white. His reaction was interrupted. "Father, don't be so surprised. People come back to life all the time." She stated hoping it sounded far more convincing to her father than it had to herself. "I had to find my way back here. I can assure you it was very difficult, so you should be proud. I only just found this place again today."

Helena moved her attention back to her patient.

"What are you doing to him?" Captain Hank asked. Despite August looking as if he was in a peaceful slumber, in the captain's mind, August could be dead.

"I'm just going to check his pulse," Helena stated, still looking at August. His black t-shirt hid his shallow exhales too well for her taste. It would have been easier to check his pulse than to see if he was breathing. Her hands were cold and August did his best not to stiffen up when Helena's chilly fingers touched his wrist.

Captain Hank leaned down, observing her actions. "Well, despite my best intentions, I'm not very good at taking care of people," her father said softly, almost as an apology for losing her.

Helena grinned, lightheartedly pushing him away. Captain Hank smiled in victory at her reaction. It was true that he spent many nights sharpening his swords as he thought about losing his daughter. His original mission had been interrupted by the pirates. He had seen the pirates take her, but never actually saw her die. He searched for her, but was never able to find her.

During his time alone, Captain Hank often began checking in with every survivor. It was his way of not only keeping a headcount, but to make sure they were not alone in grief or fear of their situation. He remembered the day he lost his ship to the pirates, when the safe environment he had cultivated for his daughter was taken from him. Helena had saved herself, while he had mourned her life. Her return surprised him and filled him with insurmountable gratitude.

"You should get some sleep," Helena instructed him. "I'll take care of August. He's, my friend."

"Alright," The captain agreed. He strained as he stood and walked away. He questioned his reality as he trudged over to his cot. Captain Hank did not want to be too far away, as he wished to witness that Helena's presence was not just one of his prophetic dreams. His dreams were often riddled with symbolism and visitations from those who could not possibly be on the ship. "Goodnight," he said loudly still in her line of sight. She waved in return.

When Helena glanced back down at August, she jumped with her hand flying to her heart. August had opened his eyes and was peering up at her from under a half-lidded gaze. "Dear, God," she whispered in a panic.

"Sorry, I'm a light sleeper, and your dad woke me up." August chuckled, but it turned into a cough.

Helena sighed. "Does your back hurt?"

He blinked, "Yes. It's stinging. Why? Is that bad? What happened to me?"

"Turn over," Helena instructed. Helena had to help August, roll over onto his side, as he could not do it himself. A small shard of broken glass was stuck in his back. August was squirming in pain, so Helena took his hand to stabilize him. "August all you have to do to reduce the pain is stop moving," she sassed him firmly with a fake smile, attempting to pacify him. Helena noticed him attempt a quick, painful grin to her in return. "It's a piece of glass." She spoke calmly, in a deeper tone than she had used before. This was the voice of a young woman going into the medical field.

The glass had cut August's shirt and his blood had seeped through. "I felt a little pain earlier," he explained to her, "I thought it was a bee sting or some kind of bug bite. Glass didn't even cross my mind."

Helena could only guess that it had happened when August had fallen after he had been rooting around in the dark. Luckily, Helena knew what she was doing and removed the small piece of glass from August's back. She attended to the small puncture meticulously, stitching, and bandaging August's wound.

Helena distracted August during the minor procedure by telling him information about his family. "I went to see if your sister was okay, but I could not find her. I am not sure where she went after we freed her. I saw the ropes were cut and the pirate captain was still there, but no Avril. So, I came back to find you, so I could ask you what room was your family staying in?" August divulged the room number. Helena got up quickly, walking away from August.

August shifted in place, while being careful with his stitches, calling after her, "You aren't gonna leave me here, are you? This is probably when the real pirates are roaming the halls. The problematic ones with hooks for hands and peg legs! Helena, I know you like near death experiences or, apparently, plain, and simple, death experiences, but don't go." As the words rolled off his tongue quickly, she could see his chest rise and fall from breathlessness. He was hoping he could convince her to stay and not leave him behind.

"Well, you didn't think of all that yourself now did you?" She called him out for his eavesdropping. "What I do or do not do – is no concern of yours - even when your family is involved. You might be interested in saving people, and it may be what my father believes you are meant to do, but I have been saving people, including myself, for months. You walked around here without a flashlight and almost got yourself killed. That's not like me. You don't know me. I will be fine. I know this place like the back of my hand. If I'm not back in twenty minutes you can say 'I told you so'." She fastened a watch around his wrist, so he could time her.

Strategically, Helena began lurking in the hallways throughout the ship, looking for room *1125*. When she spotted who she thought would be August and Avril's parents having dinner, she waited for them to be done with their meal, so she could follow them. As Helena hid in a nearby ventilation duct, she observed the Bridges. The couple appeared to be elegant, loving, and enjoying one another's company. This caused Helena to hope that these people were not the Bridges. She did not want to deliver the news about what their children were going through. However, once they got up to leave, Helena followed them through pathways she knew in the walls. Listening closely, she heard their conversation, their steps, and the direction they moved in the ship. Once they arrived outside their room, Helena took the opportunity to slip into the cabin behind the two adults. Sneakily taking one of their wallets, she checked their ID. Unfortunately, the last name listed was Bridges.

Helena revealed herself to them. They were frightened. Avril and August's parents grabbed each other's hands. "Please don't be alarmed, I found your son." Helena explained hastily with her hands up to show the two adults that she meant them no harm. In an explanatory tone, she moved her hand to her heart to show sincerity, "The ship was taken over by pirates. August and Avril ended up in the middle of things. Let me take you to your son and I promise I will do my best to bring Avril back to you."

Helena was wearing August's jacket that he had let her borrow when they went to find Avril together, which served as evidence that she knew him. Aside from her souvenir, Helena further proved her case when she revealed to them that their adjoining room was connected to a secret labyrinth in the ship. Helena planned to use this path to try to find and rescue Avril. The adults both packed a small backpack of their things, and Helena encouraged them to follow her lead.

Helena Hank realized that it was past the time she had estimated her return. She was expecting a hefty 'I told you so' from August when she got back. However, to Helena's surprise and gratification, August was sleeping peacefully.

Chapter 5

August was never interested in being right, when it came to Helena, he was only interested in her. He wanted to be next to her, yet he had watched helplessly as she walked to the other side of the room for the exit. She had reached out her hand, slid away part of the wall, and disappeared once again.

He was determined to petulantly count every second of the twenty-minute estimated time-frame he was given. Yet, it astonished him how quickly he drifted off to sleep. When he woke up, Helena was sitting beside him reading a novel. She was sitting atop a few wooden crates with her ankles crossed, swaying her legs that were not long enough to reach the floor. August looked around, trying to figure out where he was and what had happened. He saw the watch Helena had secured on his wrist and it helped to orient him. Then he asked her. "Did you make it okay?"

The book slipped from Helena's fingers into her lap. August had startled her. She picked up the book and placed it down properly, fixing the bent pages as she answered, "I did, and I brought a few people back with me." Helena pointed to August's family that had been asleep nearby, and he shot up.

Not only were his parents there, but Avril was there. August needed to know what happened to her after he saw her last, but the ache in his back reminded him of its presence. He continued to move despite the pain. It was difficult to see his family in the dimly lit room, but he knew they were surely there. Helena uncrossed her ankles, hopped down from the boxes, and stopped him from going over to them.

Turning his head with a withering glare, he said, "Thank you for safely getting them here, Helena, but I want to go to see my family."

She responded kindly despite his grateful yet sharp tone, "They're asleep, and you're injured. Let them rest, as they let you rest when they got here. Why don't you give them a bit more time to sleep?"

August wanted to protest, but the pain in his back and newly noticed hunger, convinced him otherwise. "Dinner was decent. Is the breakfast here good?" He asked. Even though he was in pain, he was well rested. Knowing his family was safe gave him the freedom of peace. However, knowing others on the ship were not so lucky weighed heavily on his mind. All of August's supposed heroic potential melted away in that moment, at the sight of a silver plate filled with his breakfast favorites. There was bacon, eggs, and potatoes that August immediately mixed into a scramble.

Helena took a bite of her food, after handing August his plate. The tine of the fork scraped against her tooth, but she was distracted from the grating sound by August's reaction to the food he was given. The brightness of his expression made her smile. They had the same food items, but August still offered her some of his, in case she was still hungry. His act of selflessness was a pleasant surprise to her, but she declined and continued to observe. August did not seem terribly brave or heroic to Helena, but he was at least kind. However, it led her to wonder if her father had the wrong guy. After all, August doubted his importance more than anyone else, maybe he was right?

Once August finished eating, Helena carefully helped him up, and allowed him to walk over to his parents and sister. Avril slept more soundly than her parents, and did not wake up upon August's arrival. His parents woke up immediately, as if his presence caused them to awaken, and they surprisingly hugged him tightly. They seemed to care greatly that he was in one piece, but Helena could not hear what they were saying as the cots were on the other side of the large room, and there were tables in between both areas, where too many others were speaking. She turned her ear toward them, straining to listen. She could guess from what she saw, that they were grateful that he was alive. Though it appeared to her that his parents would interrupt him when he tried to tell them what had happened to him. It almost seemed more important to them that August was physically okay more than emotionally.

Captain Hank interrupted the reunion, by bringing the Bridges parents some food. He briefly greeted them in a familiar way as if they somehow knew each other. Helena scrunched her forehead, as she watched Captain Hank and Mr. Bridges exchange a firm handshake before he gently hugged Mrs. Bridges. Then August's father gestured to a nearby table and took August by the shoulder wanting them to have a seat to enjoy their meal together. August stepped away from his father, pointing over to where Helena was sitting.

Helena continued to observe, harboring a wish that she had the same relationship with her parents, as August seemed to have with his. She knew it could not happen for her, even if her father did love her and wanted to protect her. Captain Hank was a man of secrets, he always was, and he always would be. Helena knew this.

Through the messy blonde pieces of her hair, which had fallen free from her high pony-tail, she watched August slowly make his way back to the medical triage area. He sat back down in the slightly inclined chair he was using previously.

Helena was curious about August's family, and watched them out of the corner of her eye. They seemed to say a unique sort of blessing before they ate their meal. Helena still could not quite make out their words, but it was not a prayer that Helena had ever seen before. Her glances ricocheted from August and back to his family across the room. At a second glance, their tradition had a sense of familial significance. August not being with them as they ate seemed to be important, as he appeared to be somewhat on edge for deciding to sit back down with Helena instead.

Now that August's family was accounted for, he began to ask Helena more questions starting with, "How do you guys have all this stuff?"

Helena watched as the wheels in August's mind were turning. She was silently listening to him ramble off his inquiries.

"Do you guys just take it from the kitchens? Do the pirates know you're here?" August chewed with his mouth open, and Helena's nose wrinkled in judgment.

She spoke with her hands mirroring her words, "Yes, they know we are here, but they don't know where."

August crumpled his forehead. "Can't they just follow the sounds and smells?"

"No, the room is soundproof." Helena pointed at the walls. The walls were covered in grey padding. August had to find a point on the wall that was not covered behind supplies to see what she meant. Helena let out a small, breathy laugh with a phrase that made her sound intimidating. "Also, they can't smell anything either."

The look in her eyes made August believe her words, that somehow, she was the reason they allegedly lost this sensation. Although it was potentially a joke. It made August slightly fear her, but her laugh granted uncertainty. August was grateful they were on the same side. He sat up straighter, with a slight struggle due to his injury. Whereas, Helena was hunching forward in comparison.

Helena knew about the pirate's threat of being able to block certain sensations, though she never came across the vile that the one pirate had shown to Avril. Helena was certainly good at dodging the pirates and saving people, but she did not know if she would be good in a fight. After all, the pirates had already taken her once.

Helena had flashes of a memory, in which, she believed that she had died. In her memory, she was underwater, but then she was laying on a clay floor and did not recall how she had gotten there. Another blink of an eye, and she seemed to be back on the boat surrounded by passengers and had to remain in hiding, as she searched for her father. It took her two months to find him, but she learned the ship's secret passageways as she lived the life of a fugitive. She stayed on the outskirts of their hiding place for a while, making sure she was not leading the pirates directly to the others in hiding. Helena learned the different routes and patterns of the ship and the pirates.

August was too busy admiring Helena to notice her solemness. She appeared to be lost in thought. He shook his head with a sigh, distracting her. He told her, "You are kind of brilliant – in a way."

Helena looked back at him, crinkling her forehead, with an expression that suggested she was unsure if it was a compliment or an insult. She asked, "In a way?"

August's voice cracked, "Yeah, how you figured out the ship, the pirates, and how all of it works." August paused. "I saw you watching my family, as if you didn't really have one like ours..." He said this carefully, as he looked to his family. His sister was still asleep, while his parents were eating and speaking amongst themselves in their children's absence.

He continued, looking back to the blonde girl, "You don't pretend to know everything, but you know a lot, and you seem to learn things quickly. I think that is pretty cool. I think you're pretty cool." He solidified with courage.

Helena made a subtle discovery in August's voice. With in inhale and a gaze downward to the floor, Helena began to believe that August's choice to return to her instead of staying with his family and the compliments he gave her, might have meant that August Bridges had a crush on her.

"Coffee?" Helena offered August suddenly, interrupting her own train of thought. She was attempting to cover the sudden panic in her voice after determining the truth of the situation. August clearly liked her, but Helena had not noticed until now and did not know what to think about that. To her knowledge, she had never experienced being 'liked' before.

"No, thank you," August politely declined, continuously being generous in letting Helena take the beverage for herself. This was enough to allow her to stop blushing; her cheeks returned to their normal creamy-tone color. August did not seem to notice the change in Helena's nerves, as she chugged the coffee rather quickly out of unease.

Helena blinked a few times, she was going to say one thing "I –" but changed her mind, shaking her head, "you probably should not be having coffee anyway. You should rest, so you can heal more quickly. I can keep an eye on your family for you. I'll let you know if Avril wakes up." Helena stood.

Once more, August wanted her to stay, so he quickly responded to her offer, with a goading sentiment, "Honestly, right now, I am content to stay here - in this room – for the rest of my life, where everyone I care about is safe."

"That's ridiculous." Helena shot down the idea, leaning back in, as he hoped that she would. "You wouldn't be able to live with yourself, and you would eventually want to get married when you're old, August." Helena spoke, crossing her arms over her chest, as she fought not to grin.

"If I ever wanted to marry anyone – then I'd marry you," he blurted out, not thinking of the repercussions of taking his prodding too far. Even if it was partially sincere, using his newfound feelings as a rebuttal was not his intention.

She protested, "No, you would not!"

"Why not?" August wondered defensively. His first declaration of affection towards a girl was not going as well as he would have hoped. August felt he typically did better in life when he was not improvising. He should have seen this reaction coming, since he had not planned his words more carefully beforehand.

"Because I wouldn't say yes." She turned away with her head held high and her nose in the air, and August caught a glimpse of Helena's smirk as she turned him down. It was almost a childlike teasing. August did not take her seriously, and thought Helena was responding in jest, yet it still stung. Now, injured in more ways than one, August felt the need to rest. As August leaned back, he attempted to coddle his own ego by mumbling to himself, "You *would* marry me."

Helena was still within earshot. "No, I wouldn't." She spun, correcting him again. Even if she had not been answering him in jest before, she did not particularly enjoy being contradicted by others herself.

"Tell me why then." August defensively insisted on knowing, even though he truly did not want an answer. He just wanted her attention, and was embarrassed that she had heard him in the first place.

"I did tell you why. It is because I would not say yes! Do you really want me to reject you more? Because I will. You're – you're..." She had stepped closer, thinking that she was going to have a clever or witty retort, but nothing came out. "Well, I don't know what you are, but I have to go. I must..." She paused trying to think of an excuse. "I must go check to see if there are any captives in the nets." Neither one of her statements were true, nor did she believe them, but now she felt as if she had to check the nets on the balcony for pirate captives.

"Fine. Go. Depart! I don't want to see you anyway," he said with a mask of anger hiding the twinges of pain.

"Depart?" Helena laughed. "You're ridiculous." She said as she left.

"So are you!" August called after her, but remained laying down on his cot.

They were both ashamed of their bickering, but neither of them would let on or apologize. While, Helena was typically good at quarreling, verbal arguments were not in August's wheelhouse. He now felt vulnerable in a way he had not before.

August could not rest. "Depart?" He mumbled in confusion over his own words. He turned on his side with his back toward his family, his face red, as he wore a frown. He wondered if Helena thought she was better than him. Maybe he just put her on the spot. August, had a heart of gold, but now he was worried his gestures had come off insincere to Helena. Maybe she thought he was not a good person, or he had somehow come across as weak or unattractive. He squeezed his eyes shut; he felt a single cool tear trickle down his hot face.

August laid there motionless, until he heard a familiar pace of footsteps. The sound interrupted his inner dialogue of self-pity and self-loathing. It was Avril, his sister. "Hey, I'm here," Avril spoke lowly, kneeling beside her brother, and she leaned her pointed chin down onto her crossed arms on the edge of his cot.

"Hey," August greeted her with a soft grin. He was grateful his sister was okay. Saving her life had been his initial focus, but in that moment, he realized he had gotten too distracted by his crush. He needed to focus on his loved ones instead of getting side-tracked.

Avril carefully turned the hilt of the dagger toward her brother. "Sorry I didn't listen to you when we were hiding in the cabinets. Here's your knife back. I just thought you might wanna know that," she apologized.

August answered, after briefly glancing down at the blade, "Thanks, but that's Helena's knife. I don't think she or dad would want me to have it."

Avril, still holding the knife, replied softly, "I don't think he would mind so much now."

The parents of the two siblings had wondered off to explore the room with Captain Hank. Whereas, Helena was working on preparations for checking the nets. She walked by August and Avril. Despite August's self-awareness of needing to concentrate, August was compelled to call after her. He wanted her to come back and stay with them, but he remained silent instead. The words seemed to be sounded out anyway, as if they were stolen from his mind. August's sister called out to Helena, "Hey wait! You forgot your knife." Avril hurried over and handed it to the English girl.

Helena smiled at Avril when she took the thin, pointed dagger and put it in a sheath that was hooked onto a belt loop around her waist. "Thanks, Avril," Helena said, and began walking away again like she had before.

August sat up too quickly as his gaze followed her as she walked away. He was attempting to see what Helena wore in her hair. It was a smaller knife that doubled as a hairpin. Overextending his posture caused August to rip open his wound. He tried to muffle the guttural moan that escaped his mouth, but Helena heard him and worriedly rushed back over. "Let's see," she gently instructed. A bruised and puss covered would was revealed when he lifted his shirt. More blood trickled down his skin. In place of where the glass had been, there was now an infection.

Helena's eyes widened, this had never happened to her before, whenever she administered first aid to people, it had never failed. Back home when she was living with her mom, she had always wanted to be a nurse or doctor. Surgery was interesting to her. Taking care of patients was, in a way, adventurous. The word, *adventurous,* defined Helena Hank. She quickly set aside her ego, but still wondered why the procedure had not worked.

"Avril," Helena lowly spoke to August's sister, "get some alcohol swabs from the first aid kit there." She nodded her head in the direction of the equipment.

August's injury was much worse than before. Avril examined what Helena was looking at, as she squeamishly handed her the requested items. "That looks bad," Avril whispered.

As soon as the alcohol swab touched his back, August passed out from the pain. Helena looked out of the corner of her eye at Avril, annoyed at the lack of pain tolerance August seemed to possess. Helena cleaned the wound more diligently than ever, stitching him meticulously once more, and cleaning the remainder of the blood on his skin with a clean white cloth. After, she hopped up onto the nearby boxes to ask Avril a question. "Tell me Avril, why does your brother not seem to care about anything? I just mean like – about saving us. Once he knew his family was fine, he just made a comment about being content. He doesn't seem to take things very seriously."

"Is that an opinion or a question? He usually cares about his friends and family more than strangers. He can be more sensitive about some topics more than others though, *definitely* more sensitive than I am." Avril lightly chuckled, quietly bashing her little brother. Despite her tendency to make light of situations, she scrunched her brow seeing that he was still unconscious. Avril gently patted his arm, before also sitting down nearby.

Helena pressed. "August said he was 'content with laying in this room for the rest of his life."

To that Avril could only laugh, "Well he does like his comfort zone."

"So, he isn't adventurous then?" Helena continued.

"He thinks he is…" Avril answered.

Helena smiled, but her joy was short-lived when she admitted, "Honestly, I can't think of anything more to do with his wound. I didn't bring any of my mom's medical books with me. It was supposed to be a short trip. My dad was just going to visit some old friends. With August hurt, it kind of makes me believe that my father was wrong about him. Maybe he isn't meant to help us. Maybe he was just symbolic or something? Like him showing up means that we might defeat the pirates soon. We are more organized now then we were in the beginning…"

With a hint of confusion in her expressive, Avril joked, "I mean, August did bring you and I together. Maybe we are supposed to save everyone. You seem to be more of a leader anyway."

Helena realized that Avril did not know about Captain Hank's dreams regarding August, but before she could explain it to her, Avril said, "By the way, I woke up to hearing you tell my brother you wouldn't marry him. So funny." Avril laughed. "Did you mean to sound so harsh?"

"Of course!" Helena responded defensively and added an explanation. "We're only seventeen. Also, he's -."

Avril stopped Helena, "Careful now, it was funny, but he's still my brother." Helena swallowed, realizing she had almost crossed a line, but Avril continued, "He's also injured, so we should probably be nice to him. He probably likes you more now that you rejected him. You're unattainable."

Helena looked at Avril wide-eyed with a blush in her cheeks, "He never said he liked me."

Avril turned her head with a playful look on her face, she quipped, "Does he have to say it? Look at your face." Avril laughed.

Avril and Helena shared stories about how they ended up on the ship, *Canadia III*, in the first place. Helena explained that she was splitting her time between her parents this summer, as she usually always stayed with her mother. Her mother was a doctor who was currently quarantined. Helena seemed very worried that her mother would be worried about her.

Whereas, the Bridges family had been visiting a nearby island to the ship's destination. Avril explained that August was forced to leave the island, but that her parents would not talk about what happened.

This intrigued Helena. Helena told Avril about the Captain's prophetic dreams. She learned that Avril had escaped the pirates, because one of them let her go. Helena wanted to know more about Avril's undercover savior, but all Avril remembered was the pirate's blue eyes and the edge of his tattoo.

Suddenly, the medical information lost in the depths of Helena's mind returned to the surface. Avril eyes widened, surprised by Helena's abrupt rambling, "Maybe if I used a topical anesthetic antibiotic, I could have scraped out the wound and then stitched him up..." Helena trailed off into her thoughts. Little did the teens realize, even stranger events were about to take place.

CHAPTER 6

August heard his mother's voice calling him out of a deep slumber, "August, wake up."

This call was followed by another sound, a man's voice stating, "Sit up, August. If you drink this, your back will heal and you will live. A great treasure, with a great risk, you may never feel like yourself again."

"What?" Was August's alarmed reaction. He remembered sitting up briefly with his eyes closed and taking a sip of water. He quickly fell back into a haze. He believed this to be a dream.

August could still hear a conversation spoken lowly. Voices were speaking about him and Helena, but he could not quite make out what was being said. There was a sense of urgency in their tone, resembling the way people spoke of him on the island. He did hear them mention Avril joining the pirates. Perhaps the rumor about Avril reached them from her escape tactics earlier, but the way they spoke worried him. The adults made it seem like Avril was going to go back to the pirates. August could not understand.

"We can't leave and we can't take him with us. There is no in and out of this for us," August heard his father's voice. It seemed to be a different voice than the one he heard earlier.

"We can't go without August. We need August..." His mother spoke, as the boy lost his fight with sleep, and drifted off into his dreams once again. He did not hear the conclusion of his parent's thoughts, nor the other voice he encountered.

When August woke up, he sat up shaking, Helena was hovering around him, constantly checking his wounds. The lights blinded him; he tightened his eyes while coughing. August groggily spoke with slight amusement in his tone, "That was a strange dream. I –"

Helena's eyes were wide as she breathlessly questioned "You dreamed?"

August blinked trying to focus on Helena's expression, but his vision was still blurry. His eyes were shuttering. It looked as if there were many people in place of the girl while the room was getting darker. He murmured. Helena held onto one of August's arms to steady him. His vision remained unfocused. "Where is my mom?" He asked the girl, but added muttering, "I'm sorry, Hilda, I don't know where I am." August seemed to be getting worse. This raised her suspicions, so she put aside the fact he had dreamed for the time being.

"August, it's Helena," she corrected him. He collapsed against her, which stunned her for a moment. Her arms closed around him, imagining this is what a hug would be like if she had ever hugged a boy her age before. This was as close as she had gotten, thinking to herself, that this would be nice under different circumstances. The only thing she did not like was a chemically sweet scent on him she had not noticed before. It was new.

Avril came up to them, and at first, she was amused until Helena mouthed to Avril, "I think he's been drugged." Eventually whispering the information to Avril so August and the others would not hear her. It was no joke. Helena's words carried an undertone of concern layered with a determination to remain calm. This action against August could only mean one thing – pirates.

Once Avril knew this was not a joke her sense of disbelief and shock began to trickle back in. "Pirates?" She deducted.

Helena had still been holding onto August, but hastily responded, "Yes, but how would they have gotten in and out of the hideout without being spotted? It – it's impossible."

"Well, don't say that," Avril exclaimed with grit.

"Why not?" Helena asked.

Avril answered, "In the movies – every time someone says that 'something is impossible' – that ends up being the very possible unbelievable thing that happens!"

Usually, Helena would be amused at Avril's remarks, but her anxiety regarding August's wellbeing impeded her to continue the conversation. However, she was distracted by August's delusional actions, and tried to get him to lay back down. He had taken to moving his arms all around trying to get back up off the bed in the triage area, so Helena was trying not to get hit by his waiving limbs. "Where are your parents, Avril?" Helena inquired with alarm.

Avril raised her brows as she realized she had not seen her parents in a long while. Were her parents now pirates? Had they joined the marching and infiltrated the safety of the hideout? The nineteen-year-old allowed herself to sit on a nearby chair to absorb the unprecedented thoughts rushing through her mind. Avril Bridges was too frightened to faint. Tears entered her eyes, while anger and sadness crept into her voice. "No – no. My parents can't be pirates."

August was now settled back down, so Helena decided to attempt to comfort her other friend. Taking a few steps over to Avril, Helena tossed her arms around her friend to console her. "It doesn't make any sense – your parents being pirates, but if they are, then it's my fault your brother is in this state. I brought your parents here."

"It's not your fault, Helena, you were trying to help," Avril said through her sniffles against Helena's shoulder. Helena gently pushed her away due to August trying to make it a group hug. Helena noticed that August was taller now than he was yesterday. She thought he must be in the middle of a growth spirt. Helena and Avril both pushed August back down for him to rest.

"Whoever your parents are now, and whoever they used to be does not matter. We can use this. If they are pirates we have to find them – it could be our ticket out of here." Helena stated as she stepped closer to Avril, slipping back the knife they exchanged earlier. "I'll bring this situation to my father's attention right now."

Helena had an idea. Perhaps if she left the Bridges children unguarded, their parents would attempt to come for them again. She stepped away from the medical triage area, at least twenty feet away.

Avril noticed Helena lift another nearby tablecloth, and could not help but wonder if all the tables had a secret doorway under them. She lifted the closest tablecloth to her to check. Her heart skipped a beat, as she heard Helena scream for help. She looked up seeing Helena dragged backward by two figures toward the staircase that was once deemed safe and secret. The two adults did not seem concerned with her attempt to fight against them.

Avril heard her friend continue to cry out for help, and then she saw the attackers, her own parents. "Stop!" Avril shrieked. The sight of her dazed and unfazed pirate parents haunted Avril. She tugged on their arms to let her friend go, pulling Helena back up to the floor from the steps below. Despite, their expressionless countenances they did what Avril instructed. Avril's eyes were wide, as she glanced at Helena. It was too easy for them to stop their actions simply because she told them to. "Could it be possible that they have been drugged, too?"

Helena simply nodded in agreement. "Yes, but they are clearly pirates now." Helena pulled a little, glass bottle of water off one of the parent's waists. She sniffed it, and it smelled chemically sweet like August, but their clothes and skin did not smell like the liquid within the bottle they carried. Helena slyly placed the bottle in one of her cargo pant pockets.

Helena stood up straighter after the altercation, as if she had an internal alarm clock set in her mind. Pushing past Avril, the English girl muttered to herself, "Time to change your brother's bandages." Avril was annoyed but also amused by Helena's obsession with first aid. Her parents had just attacked her friend, yet she was rushing away to perform more heroics. Avril looked back at her parents, and they looked at her as if they were waiting for her to say something. Raising her eyebrow she said, "Stay here. Don't move."

As Helena climbed her way back to the top of the stairway and into the room. She noticed the adult passengers in the hideout began to fall ill and pass out throughout the large room. Avril and Helena both took sharp breaths. Then without delay, the sounds of marching began again, closer than ever.

Helena saw Avril glance back to where August had been in the triage area, scared for her brother, but August was not there. The Bridges parents were also unconscious now like the other adults in the room, and were draped over the entrance down into the stairway.

"Dad?" Helena panicked, searching for him through the crowd of unconscious bodies sprawled throughout the room. Helena could not find her father. "Where is he?" She asked herself. What had happened to the adult passengers and where was her father among them? Helena was used to gatekeeping the secret stairways and tunnels, so she did not think he would have gone that way, but seeing that the Bridges had found one of her many passageways was cause for concern.

Helena stalled in her pursuit of finding her father, when she saw August. August was walking near the table that Helena had shown him earlier. He was stable. The liquid he had ingested earlier had healed him. It also caused him to look older and taller, too. Helena noticed that August was leading the teens and children to the exit that she had shown him. Her knowledge of the tunnels and passageways had been a secret before, but now the children and teens knew of them. She knew it was necessary, as the converted pirates seemed to have now infiltrated their safe haven, yet Helena felt exposed in August's decision to share it with the others. August walked toward her and Avril, closely followed by a scared little girl who would not let go of August's hand.

The freshly healed young man spoke to them, "Pirates... they are in a nearby hall; they'll find this place soon." August warned them. "Hopefully, the rest of us wake up, but we need to leave."

Zoey, a twenty-five-year-old waitress from the cruise-line, came over and scooped up the little girl in her arms. "Mark and I will accompany you guys. We'll try to help." Mark gave a shy, little wave. He appeared to be a maintenance worker who refused to become a pirate and was rescued and brought to the hideout by Captain Hank. He wore a baseball cap and hoodie to hide himself even from the others. Whereas, Zoey was blonde and friendly, but had figured out the infiltration around the same time as August. It was a generally young and small crowd that was ready to make their escape, as the adult passengers were still unconscious.

"Where are we planning to go?" Helena fiercely demanded as she was leaning quite close to August's face. Her focus narrowed as she inquired further, "And how are you suddenly perfectly healthy?"

August straightened, "Your father gave me some medicine. It made me feel wonky there for a moment. He said he got it on the island that me and my family had visited. I recognized the name – Talley something. If I seemed weird earlier that is why, but my back is virtually good as new and I can see again!" August thought Helena would be happier to know that he was better.

"We thought you were drugged." Avril hugged her brother briefly.

Helena continued to analyze August as August embraced his sister. He then grabbed a weapon that one of the other passengers handed to him. Helena noticed that August seemed to be taller, stronger, and more poised. He looked older and more attractive. Helena realized she was fighting a brewing crush. These feelings made her cringe any time she thought of anyone in that manner. She took a deep sigh, pushing the unwanted thoughts and feelings to the back of her mind.

"Where is my father? What did he give you?" She had always known her father to be unaccustomed with medicine, and this exhibited evidence to the contrary. It was suspicious to her that August and her father had knowledge that she did not.

While Helena's mind was on other things, August brought it to her attention that she had been staring at him. "Helena, I don't know. Is my back bleeding again?" August asked her in a whisper, with a subtle smile on his face, as to not embarrass her.

"No," she answered brashly and just as quietly as him. She could not hide the slight blush in her cheeks. His eyes admired her warm skin. August nodded, confidently keeping eye contact with Helena until she looked away. August was pleasantly caught off guard by her attention.

Helena turned away, pushing Avril to help her gather supplies. As Helena was packing and put the last item into the bag, she could not help but worry that the pirates must have her father. She distanced herself from her friends, making sure that no one could see her. Sitting down, hiding behind the large stacks of boxes, she simply cried until she heard someone coming. Helena was not typically the kind of young woman to cry; she was the sort to bottle up her emotions. However, Helena always knew exactly where her father was and what actions he was taking. Now, she did not know where he was and it shook her to her core. She could rally to take care of others, she could lead better than August, but without her father she was fearful.

Wiping her face, as the footsteps passed, Helena peered around the corner of the stacks. A small, glass bottle caught her attention. It was sitting where August had been recovering. It still had some liquid in it. Without a second thought, she got up and walked over to it. Helena sniffed it, it was the same scent as the bottle she now carried in her pocket. Swirling the alleged elixir her father gave to August; Helena drank the remaining liquid. She did not know why she did it or what would happen now. Her only thought was that of research. Only moments later she realized she was going to pass out. "I'm ready to go," she whispered aloud to herself as she crawled back onto the chair. Her eyesight grew dim as a wave of drowsiness set in.

Soon after, Helena was being shaken to wake up. "No!" was her cross and stubborn response as she awoke in a haze. "I have to find your brother," she said with her eyes still closed, thinking she was speaking to Avril. She was being woken up by August.

"Helena, it's me – August." August stated.

"Oh. That's good," Helena replied. "Follow the leader. I drank the rest of the liquid my dad gave you. You should know that because – you're the leader." She poked him slowly and repeatedly.

August worriedly snapped, "You drank it?"

"Yep," she quipped.

"Well, now you should try to stay close to me and Avril," August said softly, as he slid his arm behind her back, and began the process of getting Helena onto her feet. Helena opened her eyes, frightening August with the sight of two red rings illuminating her irises. August did his best not to back away from her, keeping his grip on her arms. Just as quickly, as her eyes had flashed red, they returned to normal as did Helena's aptitude.

"What are you staring at?" Helena demanded as she gave him a slight shove. August let go, but as he did Helena stumbled and he reached out for her. She grabbed onto his arms in opposition to her earlier action. She cleared her throat, and with an apologetic smirk she whispered, "Thank you."

"No, don't thank me," August answered. "Accept my apology. Captain Hank told me to dump the liquid and I did not. It's my fault you feel unsteady. You should have never been tempted. It's all coming back to me now." He paused, "Let me take your bag for you." Helena hid her blush and walked ahead of August.

August noticed that Helena looked older than she had earlier. She was taller, but not quite as tall as him. She looked to be stronger as well, even if in the moment she had lost her balance. He had the same reaction to her appearance as she had to his earlier – after they both drank the liquid. He spoke out to her in a leading question, "So how do you feel? Different in any way?"

"What are you a doctor?" She jibed, walking backwards looking at August. He held out his arm to keep her from bumping into anything in the tight space. Helena turned back around to watch where she was going, as she answered him, "Yes. I feel different. I feel angrier like every little thing is bugging me."

August caught up with her pace, pulling out a regular bottle of water. "Here." He had already gone through this and knew that water helped. Helena looked at it suspiciously, but drank it. August watched as Helena's symptoms of anger seemed to immediately deplete.

Memories were coming back to him in pieces. He recalled the voices that were speaking around him earlier, and how his eyes fluttered open to see Captain Hank. The man told August he had procured some medicine from the infirmary on the ship that originated on the nearby island, and that it would restore him at a cost.

He already felt different emotionally fearless. He did not want to reveal that he could feel the changes still evolving. His care and concern were slipping away.

August remembered what Captain Hank had said to his parents, "*We always thought that August was meant to lead, but Helena is more of a natural leader already. With our children working together I truly believe they can keep the 'fate of the flower' prophecy at bay. We are all still at risk around Avril until the union...*"

"Thanks – again." Helena interrupted August's memory, and he could hear a tone of embarrassment in her voice. He batted his eyelashes, focusing in on her grin. August simply nodded, keeping the conversation he overheard to himself.

August announced to the small group of young passengers, "Everyone, be ready to go in fifteen minutes." Then he grew quiet.

Helena noticed August's eyes after he spoke, and asked him a question, "Why did your eyes turn red just then, like a photograph with bad lighting?" She did not realize that she was the only one with the ability to see it. Helena could feel his eyes on her, and heard his hesitation to answer. "I saw it, August, don't look at me like I'm crazy," she defensively added.

"I think that drink did something to our eyes." August finally answered her question after a long pause.

"What did you see in my eyes? Were mine like yours?" An air of fear was in her countenance. The liquid in question veered outside the realm of known medicine. Helena's hands were now trembling. August pulled her into a supportive hug. Unlike earlier, this was a comforting hug – a real hug.

"I don't know, Helena, I didn't see mine." He pulled back away from her with a smile and added, "It did something to my back. You feel different and so do I, but we'll figure it out."

"I just saw it again." Helena studied his face, straining her words, as if she would scare it away if she were to speak too loudly. The liquid had not yet finished its work on Helena or August.

CHAPTER 7

Fifteen minutes went by quickly, and the young ones began to leave their haven. Avril followed closely behind her brother. August decided that everyone who was not going to be actively prepared for a possible altercation with the pirates, should go to a secondary location instead.

It was going to be a rocky road for those who decided to go after the pirates. August was worried that he was going to have to leave Helena at the secondary location because she was still half-dazed from the liquid. He wanted her to stay with him, but he knew he needed to keep her best interest in mind, especially without Captain Hank present. He had a hunch that Captain Hank would not be pleased that Helena drank the liquid. Just like with August, Helena was experiencing changes.

Avril noticed her brother was distracted by Helena's state, so she stepped in to try and engage in conversation with Helena to keep her alert. Avril linked her arm in Helena's and asked many questions, including questions about Helena's home life. "So, when you get back home one day, what is the first thing that you want to do? Sleep, raid your refrigerator, or spend time with friends?"

"I miss my mom. I think when I get home, I'm gonna make her stay home from work with me, and we will drink tea and have homemade scones. What about you?"

Avril answered, "I miss my bed. I'm gonna sleep for as long as I possibly can, and then I am going to have a double feature of my favorite movies. Then I'm gonna have cake for breakfast with a fruit cup dumped on top of the icing."

Avril could tell her brother was listening intently to her conversation with Helena. The expression on his face suggested that he wanted to join in with them, but he remained quiet.

They watched as he kneeled and removed three floorboards, and the group began to follow him to the exit of the storage room that had kept them safe for so long. They were very grateful the room had been soundproofed. For Avril, the question of why the room was soundproofed in the first place, was on her growing list of unsolved mysteries. She watched as August kept glancing at Helena, as others passed in front of them.

With a roll of her eyes, Avril sarcastically whispered to her brother, "I feel so safe."

The procession continued through the open space, down through a small corridor, and into a staff hallway. Avril had not respected her brother as much before as she did now. She thought he probably felt the same about her or at least he did before he drank the liquid. Avril's habit of using humor as a shield was still a trait that August could count on. Although, when Avril made her quip of sarcasm, this time, August barely reacted with more than a nod to her. Her expression dropped.

The small group kept moving lower into the ship. Once they were under the waterline the passengers grew quiet. Helena shared with August and Avril that these pirates had a superstition regarding being below the water line. It was bad luck for the villains. The directions of where they were traveling became like a quiet game of telephone, as the knowledge was slowly whispered throughout the group.

August noticed that Helena had barely spoken an independent word, since they started their trek, aside from the knowledge of the pirates and answering Avril's myriads of questions. Kneeling, she placed the palms of her hands on the floor. "One floor below this is safer. We should go there, but the entrance is not easy to find."

"I know you're right," August agreed. "Which is better, easy to reach or hard to retreat? We need both." August was checking to see if Helena was strong enough to fight after the liquid.

She answered, "This is a floor we can fight from if we must."

August added on to her statement, "The floor below is for everyone else and their safety."

Helena asked, "Did my father tell you what to do with that much detail?" She sounded slightly bitter.

August questioned his own right to lead, simply because he cared more about what Helena thought about him than what anyone else believed about him. He did not want to lead the group if she was going to despise him for it. It was not about what he wanted when he knew it was Captain Hank who wanted him to lead even if Helena was better suited for it. He turned away from her, deciding to believe that the tone that burned like betrayal was not intended to be reproachful. Helena was still on his side and was only upset with her father who seemingly replaced her with a dream that came true.

August walked off. He had to think about the situation. He knew he needed fresh air, or he was going to suffocate. It took him a while to get to the deck. Once he made it, all the staff members were clearly undercover pirates, and they were eyeballing August. August did not care; the courage the liquid gave him still ran through his veins.

Passing by a slushy stand on board, he heard one of them whisper, "He's not the kid we're looking for..." It made August smirk, knowing he looked different now than he had before. He walked right past them with his hands in his pockets. Because they were talking about him, he felt bold, and went up to them and asked them if there was a problem. They denied that they were talking about him, and tried to sell him an expensive slushy. This tempted August.

Reaching into his pocket, August revealed that he had a gold coin. "Will this be sufficient?" He smugly asked the men, knowing what they were, mystical pirates. They seemed to be able to smell the gold. He saw them inhale deeply and try to subtly sniffing the air. They looked as if they were thirsty dogs looking at water behind a wall of glass.

"Yes, Sir! Take whatever you'd like!" The undercover pirates answered the boy. August laughed to himself, as they prepared some beverages for him to take, as well as some treats. Perhaps he could get some real food if they truly did not recognize him.

Forgetting he had no money, having spent his gold coin, he went and ate in one of the restaurants. However, when he reached in his pocket again, another gold coin was there. It was the same kind of coin as it was before. He looked at this one a little closer. There seemed to be some worn etching on it. It was a design he could not make out. The waiter was very excited, just as the other vendors had been. It was, of course, taken as payment by the undercover pirates.

August decided to test his luck. He reached into his pocket once more, and low and behold another gold coin was prepared for him to use. However, this coinage seemed smaller.

When August returned to the group, the others had begun whispering about him and where he had gone. The rumors eventually spread to Helena. Helena did not know what August had gotten himself into. She did her best to minimize the questions and concerns others were asking her, before speaking with him herself about where he had been.

She encouraged the others about August. However, Helena purposefully left out the part about the mysterious liquid that made them both different.

Looking around the dark event room they were laying low in, she did not see August. He must have wanted to get away from those who were talking about him. However, Helena could not predict that August was beginning to not care what people thought about him.

When she found him, he was sitting alone and seemed to be doing his best to ignore people and the comments that were being made against him. Solitude seemed to suit his new attitude better. Helena took a deep breath and approached him anyway. He was tucked away in a dimly lit adjacent nook attached to the event room. His back was straight against the far wall and he was sitting on top of a cushion. August pulled a coin out of his pocket, and he was analyzing it, as Helena was analyzing him.

Helena slid in closer to him in the nook, "August?"

"Yeah?" He replied, tightly gripping the coin in the palm of his hand.

"Are you cold? I brought you a blanket." She draped it over him swiftly, as he looked away from her. She sat down next to him. Sitting side by side, they looked as if they had aged two years since they had met. Helena continued speaking when August did not respond to her. "I'm sorry about earlier. I'm just worried about my father. I'm a little on edge, and that's not even to mention that people's eyes keep eerily turning red for no reason."

That's when August pettily chimed in, being different after his exposure to the liquid, and also the mysterious coins. "Are you expecting me to throw you a pity party? Once you go home, you'll see your mom again. BOTH of my parents chose to be pirates. They chose to be a part of a group of people that kidnapped me, entrapped me, and tried to kill me multiple times. I've been hung upside down, chased, had my sister kidnapped, and I injured my back. Then I drank a suspicious liquid that was given to me by a man I knew less than twenty-four hours. That liquid was going to 'heal me' and now – mysterious gold coins with illegible markings keep popping up into my pocket one at a time." He held up the coin, showing Helena. "On top of all of that, I'm expected to be a leader, to remain calm for the sake of my sister, keep my sanity, and the highlight of my life – dealing with your problems!" He harshly snapped with a clenched jaw.

He was attempting to kickstart his feelings, but at this point August was numb. The words he spoke sounded sarcastic and cruel, even if that was not his intention. Every medication has side effects, but his experience with the liquid seemed more like a bad reaction. Captain Hank did warn him. August took a deep inhale.

Helena stared at him before responding, "You were taken and almost killed multiple times?" The surprise in her voice told August that Helena did not know he had been taken by the pirates more than once.

August shook his head. "Well, I thought the gold coins were more interesting, but yes, I have seen the marching first hand. I have been tied up and left for dead a few times. Each time – I did not join the pirates. I escaped. Then they took Avril, and that's when things changed. They only took her when she didn't believe me about the pirates. We were hiding in the cabinets in the restaurant, and she gave away our location. I guess she thought it was a prank."

August, who had put his hands back into his pockets, shook his head in exasperation. "Oh, here. I thought you might like a gold coin right now."

Helena took it from him. Helena fidgeted with the coin a few minutes before she realized that it was a gold case in the shape of a coin. She opened it. It contained some kind of powder. She closed it back to study the outside of the item closer.

"What is written on it?" The girl mumbled. August watched her, as she read, "*Half of the moon is taken by the footprints, the flower is taken by half of the moon; the sword sits in the sand until Grace eclipses the moon, and then Lence overlaps the sun...*" Helena frowned and looked at August with confusion. "What is this?"

"What do you have microscopic vision?" He asked her, as she felt his chin slightly rest on her shoulder. His glance fell on what she was observing. "Does this one say anything?"

"Um yeah it does," she answered while gesturing to it, "it's the same thing but the words *flower* and *Grace* are switched."

"What do you think it means, Helena? I couldn't even read it," August asked her.

Helena pulled the two halves of the coin apart, noticing that they had a powder inside. August leaned back away from Helena. Avril had joined them. Helena quickly snapped the pieces of the coin back together, and began to include Avril in the conversation, Helena asked her, "Have you received anything significant since you boarded the ship? Like a coin or anything?"

"No, but I did learn to make an idiot out of myself when I'm scared, and how to be a fake pirate," Avril joked, but her laugh was interrupted by a haunting sound, marching.

Chapter 8

August announced that they would now be moving those who could not fight to their safe area, but the marching sound radiated amongst the passengers, and they could barely move. August and Helena noticed that they were unaffected by the mystical marching, and this must have been another side-effect of the liquid they both drank.

"Help me lead," August whispered a small prayer to God. Then he stood up to speak to the others.

"Alright guys, this is a fight that we can lose if we don't prepare now. Prepare your minds. No noises or sights should catch us off guard. If fighting doesn't seem like it's something you can do we have a safe area. Fight with us, but please don't intrude in this battle. Neither is a wrong choice if you choose what's right for you." There were approximately fifteen in their group of fighters. Two of them decided to join the safety group after August's short speech.

"Hey," August said to Helena, after seeing that she was ready with her dagger in hand. "Make it out alive, please." August did not feel like those were the right words to say to her in the moment, but he wanted to say something just in case.

"Lead," she said to him with a smile. The two locked eyes. Helena overheard his prayer. He surmised that Helena had acquired enhanced hearing from the elixir. He was mesmerized by her sly comment.

One of the doors of the lower level's event room flew open with a bang, the pirates appeared with their swords drawn. "Come out, come out, wherever you are." The pirate captain began to taunt the children and teens to come out of hiding.

All the young ones were hiding, waiting for a clear shot at the pirates – especially the captain. This was their first time seeing the pirate captain and the black bands he wore on his arms. The more bands, the more important the pirate. He was the most important and capable pirate on the ship.

The pirate captain continued provoking the passengers, "Oh, so I guess opening this door to your 'secret safe room' won't ruffle any feathers. Helena Hank, your dear ole daddy is gonna get torched with the rest of 'em – and you won't even show your face?" The evil captain laughed, while August and Avril's parents dragged Captain Hank into the room.

Helena's eyes shown as she put a hand to her mouth, stifling a cry. August thought Helena would have had thrown her dagger at the pirate captain, but instead she put down her weapon. She was not in their sights yet, as she reached into her pocket, and pulled out the gold coin that August had handed her. August had no idea what she was doing. After having the coin in hand, Helena picked up her dagger and she walked out of hiding.

Captain Hank was thrown to the floor. He had a beeping red device tied onto his chest. "I love you." The real captain told his daughter.

"I love you." She returned the sentiment.

August could not let Helena stand against the pirates alone, especially now. While Avril was still safe in the shadows of the room with the others, August turned his focus to Helena. The other passengers were more than capable of fighting for themselves. He rushed, grabbing two dart guns stashed nearby. He threw Helena one of the additional weapons, and they proceeded to shoot at the pirate captain with darts.

With the pirate captain unconscious, August approached his own parents. It seemed as if their minds were still being controlled. He intuitively gave them each a coin not knowing why.

Hearing an explosion behind him and a blast under his feet, August jumped and covered his ears. "Avril!" August screamed. "Helena! ...Captain Hank?" He had to evaluate the room through smoke and fire. He could only feel heat. Unable to hear or feel the marching, the children and teenagers opened the doors. They were met with many more marching pirates. August figured this was the end.

The adults had woken up in the hideout and made their way to the lower level to help when they heard the intense commotion. The additional passengers began to fight the bad guys in the smoke and flames. August saw someone extinguishing the flames from the fire. That is when he spotted Helena in the clutches of a pirate. He stormed over, shoved the man with bands on his arms, knocking the rival to the floor. He leaned down and picked Helena up, and carried her out into the hallway that was now visible.

There were some passengers that did not make it out of the fight that transpired. Some were mistaken as pirates and some were trusted as passengers that were undercover pirates. It was never forgotten by those who lived.

When it was clear, the passengers were victorious. All the people on the ship that did not know what had transpired were rightfully terrified by the occurrence. It was quickly covered up in the guise of a conspiracy.

That night, after the two teenagers spent hours searching for Captain Hank and the remaining Bridges family, they slid into the control room of the ship. They had the help of a former sailor to navigate the cruise and its passengers back to safety.

August and Helena sat in silence, not accepting the potential deaths of their loved ones. Their families could have been taken by the explosion, fire, or attacks from their enemies. Instead of allowing the uncertainty to cripple them, they sat on the floor against the back of the control room peering out the window at the sea. There was a large steering wheel in the midst of an array of buttons and screens.

Helena whispered to August, "The coins you keep finding in your pockets, they contain a powder, and I was wondering if it had any medicinal benefits like the liquid does? Maybe they are connected."

"Interesting," August muttered. He still could not access the full range of his emotions due to the mysterious side effects of what was given to him. He thought about how the coins first started showing up in his pockets. When he first drank the liquid, some of it spilled on his legs. Like Helena, he wanted to know what the elixir truly was, and the only thing he could remember was the echo of the word *treasure*.

They were silent for a few minutes, as exhaustion began to weigh on their eyelids. Helena was dozing off as they watched the water below from out of the wide windows of the ship. August spoke to her as her eyes began to close, "Funny thing is, I thought you knew what all that stuff was – the liquid – the coins. I assumed you knew since you told me many stories when we first met. It feels like so long ago, even if it has only been a day or two. You knew everything. You knew more than me and more than Avril. I trusted you and your brain. You seemed special."

"Special? What do you mean?" Helena asked.

"I *know* you are special. I don't feel it anymore, but I know it. You and I drank the liquid, we see people's eyes turn red, you can hear quiet sounds and see tiny things. You are special, and for some reason so am I." He admitted to her. "Basically, we're stronger, taller, and even richer because of the gold coins. Let's face it – on top of that – you died before I met you! Your dad had dreams about me before he met me. How are *we* not special?"

"You also got kicked off that island," Helena added on.

"Yes. Exactly! Wait, how did you know about that?" August asked.

"Avril," they simultaneously answered. They both stared at the ceiling in the control room of the ship.

"Maybe we are special," Helena accepted.

"Only, I still think your dad was wrong. I don't think I'm meant to help save everyone or lead." He turned his head to look at her, "I think I'm meant to help protect you."

Later that night, after Helena went to use the bathroom, she came back into the room with a man holding a gun toward her face, alarming August and the sailor who was taking them to safety.

The strange man announced, "I want my ship back." He was not Helena's father nor was he the pirate captain, yet he claimed the ship was his.

"What do you mean *your* ship?" August stood facing them, wearing a fierce expression, as his hands were balled into fists.

"Aren't you both a little young to be running a ship?" The strange man asked him in return.

"Aren't you a little old to be threatening kids?" August stood against this new adversary, while still void of the emotions within himself. He only knew he could not let anything happen to Helena. She was his equal, his partner, and he should feel a responsibility to keep her safe.

"Well, I'm not putting down my weapon until you give me back my ship, pirates!" he opposed.

"Pirates?" Helena and August questioned him in unison.

August looked at the sailor by the wheel and back to the threat. "We're not pirates. We just saved this ship. Most of the pirates are - gone - or back to being regular passengers.

Now, put down your weapon and tell us who you really are," August demanded confidently, or at least he sounded confident.

The unusual man, who was not making sense, set down his weapon. August carefully scooted next to Helena, scooped her into his arms, and pulled her away from the man while shooting him a glare. August looked Helena in the eyes, as he held her. Helena was not typically someone who needed to be saved, but in this situation, there was no way around it. August saw his role on this ship as the protector of Helena Hank. If he could help her, he would. She nodded at him that she was okay. His attention reverted to the threat.

"I'm Captain Sherman Livingstone. I'm the Captain of this ship," the man testified. August and Helena looked at each other and back at the man. This was new.

"My father is the captain of this ship," Helena answered him, as she was still holding onto August.

"No! He is the one who trapped me in the bottom of the ship! I only just escaped when the battle took place. Why would you think he was the captain? He's a liar." Sherman Livingstone recoiled.

Helena mumbled and began to step toward him, but August held onto her arms. "He's a liar? You're a liar." Helena seethed.

"I'm not!" The man verbally sparred back. "Nothing would stop your father from going after me. Months ago, and then again today."

Helena shook her head. "He either had a reason or you have the wrong man. Don't you dare call my father a liar ever again! Hear me?" Her angry words echoed, as she visibly fought back her tears. August felt a pang in his chest at this display of emotion.

The man responded to Helena, "I won't call him a liar again, Sweetie, but he did take my boat. This ship belongs to me. Where is your father? I would like to know why he kidnapped me, just as much as you would like to know. He did tell me he needed to save the passengers from the pirates. I just assumed you were the pirates."

Helena looked him up and down. "That sounds more like him, but it still does not explain why he would have brought me along on a work trip as a captain though...I'm his daughter he would not have put me in that kind of danger."

"Well, why don't we find out then?" Livingstone pushed.

"He's lost, I'm not sure if he made it out..." she trailed off.

Livingstone empathetically answered, "I'm sorry."

"Thank you," she choked.

August found himself unable to navigate the emotional angles that everyone else was feeling. He questioned the man flatly, "Are you sure Captain Hank didn't tell you anything else, Captain Livingstone?"

"He only ever said anything about saving the passengers and protecting the treasures. I still don't know what that meant. Now if you'll excuse me, I'm going to get back to steering this ship to its original destination. Also, thank you, for calling me Captain again." The man answered.

August faked a sincere smile, since he could not feel his emotions and cognitively knew this was when he should smile. Yet, he also knew calling this man a captain would sting like betrayal in Helena's ears. He turned to Helena, still holding her tightly. The newcomer clearly made her uncomfortable, but August gave another performance of what he wanted his face to portray. He rolled his eyes at the words, and offered her a smirk to show to her that he was still on her side.

As the sailor and other captain discussed their course, Helena whispered to August. "Treasure?" He never told me anything about a treasure."

August raised an eyebrow in sarcasm. "Well, what are a group of pirates doing marching around a ship if there isn't a treasure involved?"

"I know we don't know what or where it is, but my dad may have died protecting this treasure. If my dad felt that it was worth his life, I think we need to protect that treasure, too," Helena stoically stated.

August suggested with the slightest twinge of excitement in his voice, "We will have to find it first. If there is a treasure, there must be a map."

CHAPTER 9

Aside from her mother back home, Helena had no one left but August. The fact that her mother might think she was dead, motivated Helena to contact her. She wanted to talk to her mom before taking any further action with August toward an unknown treasure. Helena found the ship's phone, walked over to the wall it hung on, and she made a call. Helena called home. August left the room to give her privacy and Captain Livingstone and the other sailor followed his lead.

"Mom?" Helena questioned. "Mom!" She exclaimed as she heard her mother's joyful voice on the other end of the call. "I'm alive, I am okay, but the ship was attacked." The unbearable moment came where she had to tell her mother that she could not find her father and did not believe that he made it. Her parents were not terribly close anymore, but it was quite despairing news all the same. She decided that she would spare her mother the details of the bomb and the pirates. It was a strange and silent kind of conversation after, with tears shed by her mother.

"I told him it was too dangerous, that it was crazy, and he didn't know what he was doing," Helena's mother's voice trembled as she responded to her daughter. "Honey, I love you, I miss you, but I have to tell you the truth about something." *The truth* sounded like sweet, beautiful relief to Helena's ears, even if the accompanying words felt like broken shards of glass being stabbed in her heart. Helena had not realized how weak she was, until her mother started speaking to her. Now she felt stronger physically and emotionally in contrast. Rejuvenation filled her heart, and made her ready to face the world again. Then once she stopped smiling, she focused on the words that her mother was saying. "There was never a quarantined facility, Helena, I was not at work. We just told you that so you wouldn't worry about what you and your father were about to do..." Helena gulped as she listened. "You went on that ship to protect something very *valuable* to get back what the pirates had stolen. He did not know how many pirates would be involved, but we got the call, and it had to be you two – to protect the treasure."

"The treasure?" Helena questioned knowingly.

"The Talley Gulf Treasure," was her mother's answer, and in a dreary manner added, "it has to be protected."

"What do we know about it? Why do we know about it? What is it? Are there any clues?" Helena asked her mother intently.

"We know about it – because we owned part of it. We never knew what it was or at least I didn't. Your father had all the answers and knew all the secrets. All you need to know is that your father would not have died protecting it, if he wasn't sure that it was worth dying for... but you mattered more to him than the treasure. I can promise you that. He would not have put you in that kind of danger unless he knew that you were going to make it out alive. He told me – you and Augustine were the real protectors of the treasure. Did you meet Augustine Bridges?" Her mother asked her in a serious tone.

Something in Helena's intuition barely made her answer and so she answered with a lie, "Uh - no."

"If you find him, stay close to him. Helena, he will keep you safe," said her mom.

"Why is he so special?" Helena asked.

There was a long pause before her mother answered, "His ancestral line is closely linked to the treasure. He was born on the same island the treasure is from, but you have to know, you are also special to the treasure, too. Your father insisted that you were. I can't tell you anything else."

"Well, do you know where the treasure is now – if it's not on the ship where dad thought it was? Did dad mention anywhere else it could be where the pirates may have hidden it?" She asked.

"I don't know, but there was historically a royal map. If the pirates got ahold of the treasure they would have taken the ship back to the source of the treasure – Talley Gulf Island," she concluded through fresh static.

"Where is it?" Helena questioned.

"It's breaking up, I love you!" Her Mom quickly announced.

"I love you," Helena hurriedly stated.

"Be safe! Remember find and stay close to..." it cut off before her mother could finish speaking.

"August," Helena whispered to herself, slamming the phone back on the wall in a saddened rage. What she always did when she was emotional was completely uncanny. Helena recalled drinking August's medicine. She recalled how she would always sneak into her mom's lab when they were on lockdown. Her reckless nature was what led her mom to push for Helena to go with her father on this trip. Her intrusive thoughts always won. Somehow, she knew she would come out okay if she risked everything. Helena leaned against the boat's control panel. Just as it always did, her intuitive anger brought her luck. The buttons she had pressed brought a map onto the screen.

What the screen showed was not the mainland, but the island that the Bridges family had gone out of their way to visit. This was the island that Avril had told her about, Talley Gulf Island.

Helena pressed the touchscreen pad that popped up, typing in a code to access its navigation system. She was not sure it would work, but guessed that the password was her name and she was incorrect. Tilting her head, a sense of certainty entered her mind. Her father seemed to put his faith in August. Again, she tried but this time using the word, *August*, and it was correct. She set their course from the mainland to Talley Gulf Island.

Little did Helena know, that much like the pirate's marching, only those that knew of the island could see the island. It would have been impossible for the navigation system to get them directly to Talley Gulf Island without her having already known of it through Avril and August.

Even though Helena was going to find and protect the treasure for her parents, she could not shake the understanding that they had lied to her. Her father had told her he was the captain of this ship, and he was never truly the captain. The sudden holes in all his words to her finally surfaced. The thoughts and memories dumbfounded Helena Hank. Trust that had been held up by the strong bonds of a lifetime had been broken. Betrayal went back through the years and unlaced many moments of truth and honesty Captain Hank had spoken to his daughter. *Captain* Hank was not even real; he was just a character.

Helena pulled on the door and stomped her feet in every step she took, but her heart was soft and it was hurting. This was the kind of anger that was not as lucky for her, it was the kind that was more debilitating.

Why not stop? Her father had lied about being the captain, and it bothered her so much it made her question continuing the trek for the treasure. However, Helena thought of her mother and the words she spoke about August. Therefore, she decided concretely in her mind that she was going to stay with August Bridges and travel to Talley Gulf Island.

Helena walked down the hallway as if she were the new captain, keeping it hidden that she was the one directing their course. She was going to be calling all the shots one way or another. Her head was held high, her shoulders were back, and she carried herself with an air of strength. When she knew more information than others, she always felt superior to them. Stomps, steps, and paces were taken in stride as she made her way to a lounge area.

The room was originally a staff lounge that was not for the passengers, but none of that mattered anymore. It was open to everyone after the battle. The survivors went where they wanted to go. The door squeaked as Helena slowly opened it.

August and Captain Livingstone looked up. August, who had been sitting crisscross applesauce on the floor, stood to his feet and walked up to Helena. He whispered like he still pictured her as a wounded butterfly even though she knew she was the opposite. August Bridges did not seem to notice the change in Helena's countenance.

"Hey, Helena, what happened in there? How did it go?" He rubbed her arm soothingly, but his new apathetic nature left the moment cold. August did not notice he touched her arm. He was acting off muscle memory, for how he treated those he cared about before. It was a typical sympathetic action for him to take.

"We have a stop to make on an island that was important to my dad. It's my way of paying my respects – I guess. It needs to be done," Helena sounded strong, but her voice grew weaker as she tried to be more convincing.

Helena had not anticipated bringing Captain Livingstone in on their plan, but he and August glanced at one another and agreed to help her get to Talley Gulf Island. However, they did not know that they were already on course for it. "The ship is heading that way as we speak," she said, which caused Captain Livingstone to leave the lounge area immediately.

Helena sat down, sighing deeply. "Sitting down is something I consider a luxury these days," she joked, expecting August to laugh as well. The expression on his face seemed to indicate that something had pierced through his emotionless predicament and was bothering him.

"What's wrong?" Helena asked him hastily.

"What's wrong? You! To change the ship's course without telling me first? I thought we were partners. I can't feel anything, and I'm still trying to be me – for you. I don't think you get that the planet doesn't revolve around you, Helena Hank, Princess of Mystery," he snapped, veering close to an outburst.

Helena shot up and looked him directly in the eyes, but she cooly said, "First of all, I am not an idiot, and I do not believe the world revolves around me. I do, however, think we are special – just like you said earlier and I was just exploring that. Also, Princess of Mystery? I do not know what that is or what it means, but I'll take it as a compliment."

"That wasn't a compliment..." August took a step toward her, and he pushed a strand of her hair behind her ear. When he touched her, he felt a twinge in his heart.

August did not know the effect he had on Helena as he leaned in to whisper in her ear, "This is a compliment. You are more beautiful than any possible treasure."

Temperamentally, Helena was torn by whether she wanted to remain or bolt. Her blood pressure had increased. Running away was her habit, but this time she truly wanted to stay. Against her nature, she remained completely still admiring the color of his eyes. She had missed this detail before, as the shade had not changed from the liquid. His eyes were still deep turquoise, and she was still a cool-toned blonde.

Helena watched as August admired each strand of her hair that moved out from between his fingers. He was breathing so calmly, and he smelled like mandarins. Helena did not fix the strands after he passed his fingers through her hair, as she did not dare to budge even if they had fallen out of place. It crossed Helena's mind that August was torturing her by showing her what she could not have, as she had already told him she would never marry him. Helena wanted to change her mind.

"Hold on," She snapped, grabbing him by both arms tightly. August stood completely still. "We must get back to the task at hand. You were right. We must protect that treasure, and my mom thinks it has something to do with your family. My dad said you were special. Whether he was an imposter or not, you are still important. I just thought you should know. Talley Gulf Island is where we look for the treasure." Helena smiled a cunning smile.

To August Bridges it seemed that in this moment, it was as close to Helena Hank as he would ever get romantically.

He looked around. His expression danced from amusement, seriousness, and sadness. This was the first real emotion he had displayed in a while.

August clarified, "What I said to you just now – had nothing to do with the treasure. I don't care if the treasure has anything to do with my family or even if it belongs to me. I certainly don't care where it is right now. You do realize I was trying to tell you that you're beautiful, right?" He remained still, his gaze traveling across her face. "I don't feel anything when I'm away from you. I still care about you. Tell me something, Helena. What is going on inside your head? I can't keep waiting to know what you're thinking."

"No one is forcing you to wait," she answered, yet her words opposed what her heart believed.

"Helena..." He pressed, but she remained steadfast.

August walked away, as the lack of words started to burn in his heart. Was that what it was like for him to feel? He could not remember. It felt the way an arm feels after cutting off the circulation and then trying to wake it up – like pins and needles.

Helena's face felt warm, and her heart was pounding. She was wiping away tears from her eyes as quickly as they were forming. Her thoughts were boiling in her mind. Was she really the way that August had described her as if she thought the planet revolved around her? Was his opinion about her right?

Helena saw a mirror across the room, walked over to it, and examined herself. Helena said to her reflection, "You are stronger than people think." She turned her head and looked at herself in the mirror. Instead of having a moment of self-discovery internally, it became a moment of self-discovery externally. As she spoke, her irises turned red. Helena repeated the same sentence over again to herself, and the redness transpired once more. This made her think, and she said, "You aren't strong." Nothing happened to her eyes. Then she said, "You are a lot weaker than people think you are." She saw the red ring again. Lastly, she said, "My hair is purple." This was when she understood that when she drank the liquid it gave her the ability to see if people were lying or telling the truth!

She grabbed hold of each side of the mirror with both hands, looking closely at her eyes. She continued to test it repeatedly. A triumphant smile spread across her face. This meant she could not be hurt by deception ever again. Her realization put August's interrogation into a new light. The best part was that now she knew for a fact that August was a truthful person and a worthy partner. It also meant that they could trust Captain Livingstone.

"August." Helena closed her eyes and whispered to herself. She could picture his happiness of her discovery in her mind. She did not know where she was going to look for August on the ship, but she was going to find him. Losing him would make everything they went through together a waste of time.

Just as she was about to leave, there was a loud creaking inside the walls of the room she was in. Helena recognized the sound, so she ran and hid in one of the cabinets. This cabinet was just big enough for her to sit inside with her legs curled up. Then she heard the floor on the outside of the cabinet being smashed through. Voices were saying they had to find August. Were they remnant pirates?

Helena put a hand to her mouth as she listened. All the people, pirates, or whoever was breaking through had now gone, except for one, who was left to search the room. They were very close, and Helena felt that this time she was going to be found. She said a quick prayer, just as she observed August had done before the pirates attacked them.

The cabinet door opened with a great surprise. "Dad!" Helena breathlessly squealed, as she jumped into her father's embrace.

"Helena," he said squeezing her tightly until she pulled away and they both sat on the floor outside the open cabinet door.

"Why did you lie to me? You could have just told me what you were really doing on this ship," she said as she dried her tears once more.

"I was protecting you," he protested. He figured her tears were from fear, rather than being happy about seeing him. "If you had known about all the dangers involved, you would not have let me do what needed to be done. Just like you and your secret hallways," he chuckled and Helena laughed with him as she wiped her cheeks. "August's sister Avril told me about your secret passageways, but I already knew. I'm proud of you anyway. Also, I'm sorry I didn't tell you what we really came all this way to do." He hugged his daughter again.

"August left here a few minutes ago, so he shouldn't be far." Helena told him.

"Ah yes, Augustine," her father said, pulling back from their hug and standing to his feet. He held out his hand to help his daughter up off the floor. "So, tell me, Helena, what do you think of him – August?" he asked frankly.

"Passionate," she began, which concerned her father, but she added, "about everything."

"Everything? Wow. That is a very passionate person," Captain Hank joked. Helena laughed.

"What do you think he is most passionate about?" He continued his inquisition as the two of them walked into the hallway. "His family, religion, or the treasure?"

"Well, yes, all of the above and…" Helena replied. They looked down the hallway into the control room, and saw the people that had broken through the floor. They were all gathered and August was already talking to them about the plan to visit the island. Helena and Captain Hank stopped walking. "And me," Helena concluded.

Captain Hank took her in his arms and gave her a big hug, and this time he held on to her a bit longer. He said quietly, "Let me guess, you are just too tough for him."

"No, it's more like I'm afraid of being too weak," she admitted.

"Helena, let me tell you something I learned from your mother. Love is the strongest bit of toughness a person can have. By letting someone you love – love you back – you make yourself stronger. When you are old enough, and your love is real, strong, and enduring you will be able to navigate the toughest storms in life. The right partner will make your life easier." Captain Hank sighed. "If August is passionate about you, he will not be able to let you go. If love is strong enough it will last."

"The best outcome of unrequited love is respect then?" She questioned him.

"Don't mess with an already broken heart," he answered her. "Especially if you're the one who broke it."

He gave his daughter a sly smile, as he understood her intent well enough.

She smiled and she was able to forgive her father, at least a little bit. "I didn't mean to break it," she answered softly. "I'm just tired." Helena had a habit of declaring she was tired whenever she was sad, but that did not stop her parents from always supporting her need for rest.

Suddenly, the ship stopped moving. Helena saw August following behind the group of people that had been searching for him, but as the others went around the corner out of her sight, August stopped to re-tie his shoelaces.

Helena looked both ways and ran up to August calling his name, "August."

August looked directly up at Helena when he heard her voice. He smiled. It seemed instinctive as she jumped in his arms. Picking her up with a wide smile, he spun her around. August leaned toward her, and was going to kiss her, but he got too nervous and he wanted to hear what she had to say first, or at least that was the excuse he told himself.

Helena was finally allowing herself to live in the moment. Feeling his face inch closer to her own, she saw the seriousness fused with joy in his eyes, and was prepared to be kissed. She noticed the way he pulled back.

"What are you doing?" he asked her, his arms still wrapped around her.

"I didn't want you to walk away earlier. I just didn't really have the strength to say what I wanted to say to you. When you walked away, I found my dad! I know that's beside the point but–"

"That's great," August interrupted her with a manufactured smile. He could feel the pins and needles again, as he tried once more to feel his emotions. However, he knew he should be happy, and the sensation of pins and needles alerted him that he cared.

"I like you, okay?" She admitted as she pulled away from him, while he watched her fidget with her hair.

"Okay," he answered, while shifting his wide smile to a grin, to make Helena more comfortable, "That's all I wanted to know." August attempted to make Helena feel safe in her declaration. He could feel a greater twinge of happiness in his heart, and he was curious if the rest of his emotions would return with time.

August and Helena embarked on the trek for the treasure. The conclusion that they needed to go on this adventure together, cemented their connection. After everything that transpired, they realized they truly were partners. The first place they needed to look was the island where all of August's troubles began, Talley Gulf Island.

CHAPTER 10

Talley Gulf Island was originally inhabited by two great families that took care of the land. Their property split apart from the mainland and became an island. One of the great families volunteered to remain on the island to protect it from the changes in sea level, earthquakes, and the changes of the natural geography they were experiencing. Whereas, the other family would have to stay on the mainland during the continuing split. This would ensure the survival of both their homes and people. Both were difficult tasks, as one family had to acclimate to the mainland and the other had to ensure their home was not destroyed. In their hearts each group believed their job was more important and more honorable than the other's.

For a long time, they did not know the outcome of each other's fates. The islanders built a bridge that connected with the mainland to bring the other family back home. Once this was completed, they were in communication again and interacted with the outside world and sometimes married leaders from the mainland and other countries.

Those who remained on the island throughout the split coexisted with the treasures of the land. They were familiar with its properties and were not drastically affected by the treasures that grew like plants from seeds on the island. This was the Augustine family. These were the bridge makers. The original dwellers were synonymous with the treasures. They did not need them, and were considered natural beauties.

Those who had lived on the mainland during the divide and returned to the island after the landmasses had settled, were unharmed. The island harbored many treasures which held differing abilities. However, when they later exposed their new family members from the outside world to the treasures of the island, their families grew ill and exhibited changes in appearance and behavior. Many of those affected were stronger and more alluring now.

Similarly, those were born on the island, but left for the mainland were also susceptible to the complexities of the outside world. The friends, allies, and lives of all the mainlanders needed the treasures from the island for medicinal purposes. Whereas, their new family members did not know the cost of using the same treasures without having been exposed to them from birth.

Many of those who were not born on the island eventually left. They had lost their emotions. The familial ties that brought them to the island were severed from the exposure to the treasure. The ones who brought the outsiders to the island, left with them once more for the mainland. They followed their emotionless loved ones changed by the island's properties.

Those who remained on the island after living on the mainland, aligned themselves against the bridge makers and made their own family the royals of the island. This family was the Corazana family. This led to there being two lines of royalty whose origins were still both tied to the island.

Hundreds of years of history divided the two families further. More mystical treasures appeared throughout the island over time, and the families warred over them. The bridge itself was eventually destroyed as were many other beautiful sights on the island, as the monarchies were dismantled. The Corazana family were still considered royals from some of the modern inhabitants of the island. However, from that same line, the pirates were also born. Whereas, the bridge makers had family that remained throughout the island to protect it, while many of them were forced to leave the island from the dangerous threats of the pirates. The members of the Bridges family relocated around the globe.

Talley Gulf Island was an island not easily found, and was considered a lost civilization. Despite this title, they had a combination of modern and ancient technologies, as it was still possible to come and go from the lost land of the European tribes that lived there. The only way to find the island was to already know of its existence.

For August, seeing Talley Gulf Island for the first time almost felt like the memory of a reoccurring dream he had when he was younger. It was the same one he had again on the ship – a dream where someone stole a marigold from him under a half-moon.

As he began to exit the ship, he looked back to see Helena following his lead. She had tilted her face up to see the sun. He watched as she took a deep inhale of fresh air, letting the rays of light brush over her face. August's breath caught in his throat as he observed her. He had never seen her look as radiant as she did in the sunlight, as the sunshine seemed to cultivate a grin on her face. August turned back to watch where he was walking, but the image of Helena in the sunlight stayed present in the forefront of his mind.

There was a celebration taking place on the island as they arrived. As the festivities took place, the acting leader of Talley gulf Island, Talbasta, greeted Helena and August as they stepped off the ship. Talbasta had dark turquoise eyes, hallow cheeks, and tan skin. August evaluated the man, as he looked familiar.

The people cheered and welcomed the two as they walked. No one explained why they were so ecstatic, especially since August had already been made to leave once before. They must not have recognized him since his transformation.

Talbasta called Helena 'Grace' and August 'Lence' but he never told them why, no matter how many times they tried to ask him. However, August recognized the names from the words he had overheard the last time he was on the island. They kept walking past the same places that August had walked with his family before, but this was a different crowd. No one was whispering about him, and he could not help but wonder why.

Talbasta took Helena and August to his home, separating them from the others to speak with them privately. His home was a beautiful, two-story clay space with carefully crafted open windows. It looked out of place in a forest, but had a mystical feel to it.

"Coffee?" Talbasta, the leader, asked them with very clear English.

"No thank you," August answered.

While Helena said, "Yes, please, thank you."

With a grin, Talbasta blew on the white rolls of steam billowing from his black coffee. "You two are different than I thought you would be. Come, follow me. I have something I must show you." He looked out the window and saw that the sun was beginning to set. "Hurry, you must come now," he repeated.

He brought them to the end of the hallway which led to a winding, clay staircase. "Come up here," he said.

They cautiously followed, after exchanging a look between themselves. "Look up, that round hole in the ceiling reveals the sky. The full prophecy predicted your arrival here today." The man giddily spoke.

August warily glanced at Helena, as he did not trust this stranger, but knew this man was the leader of Talley Gulf Island and had information they needed about the treasure. His smile was triggering a distant memory for August; he knew that they had met before, but he did not know how or where.

Talbasta continued, "The prophecy seems incorrect about your personalities. You seem to be the opposite of what you were supposed to be, but it was right about your arrival. You might not feel ready for what lies ahead, but it is the will of God." Confusion rang in the room. "The difficulties you have overcome to get here, they do not matter. Once the sun goes down, you will see what you cannot yet see during the day. The countdown will begin."

Helena inquisitively asked, "As vague as that sounds… what does that mean?"

Talbasta looked at her with a smile. "Grace, it is engraved on our currency amongst other things." He bowed his head to Helena.

"So, we have to wait til sundown?" August confirmed.

"As of now, yes. In the upcoming days, hopefully, you will see at all times." Talbasta responded.

"Fun," Helena stated sarcastically, which reminded August of Avril. He perceived her unease in the situation.

"What does the phrase on the coin mean? I never understood it." August attempted to push for a reply.

"It means *solution*…" Talbasta answered.

August saw Helena's eyes grow wide. The coins were a solution; the powder in the coins must have helped create the medicine that they both took. August figured that this revelation meant that this island could literally grow these coins like seeds from a plant. This must be the treasure they were meant to find and protect.

"Right now, you have not used enough treasure to enact your destinies. However, under the right moon, you will be able to see it tonight. This is only the beginning of the prophecy. I'll be back in time for sunset, as you should both take this time in silence for prayer, meditation, and solution." Talbasta turned, walking away from them in the unfamiliar attic, and began to descend the clay, circular staircase.

"Where are you going?" Helena called after Talbasta.

"To prepare. Whenever a ship is docked near this island, the pirates come and try to take it. We need that ship, my *friends*. Take this time to prepare your minds," he answered, bowing his head slightly and exiting the room.

August smiled, trusting Talbasta. The memory of looking up at the man's smile returned to August's mind. He must have been a young child when he knew Talbasta, and even though August could not remember further details, he finally felt safe again. Maybe this was the family friend his parents were going to visit. He turned to Helena as Talbasta left. "Don't worry. We'll be fine." They sat together thinking and preparing as the sun set.

While Talbasta was walking to the ship, past the celebrating locals, he saw a few folks that were not celebrating. He knew pirates when he saw them, and he knew that he was being followed.

As he walked, trying to maintain a calm countenance he recalled his childhood on the island. His parents had protected the Talley Guld Treasure when he was young. Playing in the house was never an option, so he was always outside unless it was mealtime. His parent's titles were Grace and Lence, as were all the protectors of the treasure, as the responsibility to protect the treasure was their position's inheritance.

One day, a man called Amos Nector came to Talbasta's home asking for money. They had none to give the man, but spare coins from the remainder of the royal treasure they protected. They gave him seven gold coins, and he asked for five extra coins. They asked the man why he asked for more? His answered was that he wanted one for every month of the year, and Grace and Lence gave the man what he desired.

The moment the gold touched Amos's fingers; his pirate nature came alive. He was not born a pirate, but both of his parents had been pirates. They had the ability to sniff out gold from thousands of miles away due to their interaction with the properties that this island possessed. Amos Nector now had the same scent of piracy.

A gold coin from everyone he met became Amos Nector's demand. A problem arose from his plan, for no other on the island had any spare gold and most had no gold or riches at all.

The next year Amos Nector came back to find Grace, Lence, and Talbasta. They invited him into their home, once more, and this time offered him a meal. He excused himself from the table to search for the gold and he found some of the hidden treasure in their home. He could not see it, but could smell it. Stuffing his pockets with gold, he returned to dinner. When he left with the gold, no one knew it, but two-year-old Talbasta found one of the coins the man dropped and was playing with it. Amos Nector's sins were found out. The Lence and Grace went after the pirate, insisting for him to return the stolen items, but it was too late. When they did find him Nector had spent the spoils of his raid already.

"To fight for this land – he gets what he gets," Lence said to Grace, to which she nodded. The thief's skin turned, producing a layer of dust he could never wash away, and prevented him from stealing and getting away with his crimes.

"He will never see the shine of gold in his own hands again," Grace noted. Truly, Amos Nector, could only smell gold he could no longer see it at all, even when it was in his hands. He could only see the dust inside the Talley Gulf coins.

The protectors were not allowed to curse anyone under their sworn duty, but banishment was acceptable. Therefore, Amos Nector was banished from the island, but not without threatening two-year-old Talbasta. "Mark my words, family. I considered you friends until now. Your son will die by my hand. I will kill him, and will come to his house when you two are dead and gone. The next protectors won't even be old enough to stop me. I will take the real treasure, not simply the gold droppings from it. I will do it without my sight, and I will squander it around the world. I will enjoy it, and those in my crew will enjoy it, and there will no longer be anyone or anything to protect it."

Now, because of Talbasta's parents' choice to banish Amos Nector. Amos Nector went to live on the sea, as a pirate. Fear for their son aged Lence and Grace, and they died when Talbasta was fourteen. This was the same year that Augustine Bridges was born.

Growing up, Talbasta had to secure what he knew of his parent's legacy. It was his responsibility to keep the treasures safe until the next protectors were appointed. It was not an easy job. Talbasta had twelve trunks of gold hidden in his otherwise empty attic. There were also different loose treasures scattered on the island. All, except one, were in danger of being taken by the pirates, with the royal map being lost to time and history.

News reached Talbasta that a man named Amos Nector had a son, and Ammon was his name. Ammon had grown up cruel, spiteful, and mean. He was a true pirate, as shown in his actions. Not a soul could stand in his way and live to tell the tale, unless he robbed them or committed horrors against them, or worse they would be forced to join his gang of pirates. He also knew his father, Amos Nector wanted Talbasta dead.

Talbasta grew wise in knowing how to use some of the treasures to his advantage. However, this meant the treasure was in constant danger of being taken. As much as Talbasta thought and assumed he knew about the treasure, he knew very little about it aside from how to save himself. His parents had known less about the treasure than other protectors. Much of the history had been burned to the ground with the old royal castle, before their time. However, they had been the only ones qualified to take care of it.

In Talbasta's time, he was supposed to find the next protectors, but until now he had not succeeded. It was a big world, and where would he begin searching?

He invested his time in learning about their island's history in hopes that he would make a difference in a way he was never meant to. This led him to the discovery of a prophecy.

"Half of the moon is taken by the footprints, the flower is taken by half of the moon; the sword sits in the sand until the sun eclipses the moon, and then Lence overlaps the sun..." It was an excerpt from the full prophecy. He made it his mission to search for the full edition, but only found different variations of the same passage. Some of the findings switch the word *sun* and *Grace*, while others interchanged the words *flower, April, and marigold.* The different translations seemed to come from the original two families of the island that parted ways when the island was created.

Talbasta carefully met with a trustworthy man who called himself Captain Hank. Captain Hank used to be an honorary captain in the Talley Gulf Island's Arms. He was best friend's with Talbasta's uncle. Talbasta asked him for his help. Captain Hank agreed to take the treasure and the precise instructions that went with it to keep it hidden. Captain Hank loaded the one treasure chest into his truck and carted it away.

Captain Seth Hank mentioned his daughter Helena Grace Hank to Talbasta. He told him that he was afraid that if she knew what he was doing, her light would dim from the danger. He told Talbasta that was why he was not telling Helena what they were doing because he needed to protect her from the prophecy. If he could act in her stead he would.

"Trust me, Hank, Helena is the reason the treasure must go with you. I will tell you everything you don't already know before you leave," Talbasta told him, already aware of Helena being on the ship that the trunk would be loaded onto. "It is the first step."

He told Captain Hank about the treasure and his parentage. He explained that his parents came from different parts of the world and were married. The protectors were meant to be married at some point. It did not need to take place until they were older, so long as they worked together and stayed together for the protection of the people, treasure, and prophecies. This part concerned the protective father, as he knew his daughter wanted to be a surgeon.

Talbasta explained in no uncertain terms to watch for a boy named Lence. This was one of August's middle names, which was a surname passed down from his mother's side. Talbasta could tell this bothered Captain Hank, as if he already knew who it was. Talbasta further explained that he believed Helena to be the next protector of the treasure, along with this boy whom he did not know how to find. However, he would not be surprised if Helena would find him herself, as the protectors would always eventually meet with or without interference.

"If anything, bad happens to my daughter, I will kill you myself," Captain Hank stated.

"It isn't my first death threat, Captain," Talbasta quipped. "Nothing will happen to your daughter, but the rest of us unclear."

H ank begrudgingly smirked knowing whatever they wanted to do in life, it would most likely always bring Helena back to August, to the island, and to the treasure.

It was the selfish nature of how the island and treasure worked. It thought itself more important than human life.

Talbasta had only ever opened one of the trunks himself, and that was the one he wanted Captain Hank to take with him. It was not the main treasure. However, he did explain to Hank that it was water. He had Captain Hank take a sip of the water, and it tasted like sugar. The water was from the inside of a blue cave on the island. It was ocean water, filtered through the cave by the rarest stones on earth. The stones were so strong and ingrained in the cave, that no man could loosen them. The water would sharpen the mind and the senses. This was why it was too dangerous for the pirates to find the water. It was not the only treasure of its kind on earth, but the only kind humans had reached to use for their benefit.

The history of the Talley Gulf Treasure that Captain Hank was responsible for was rambled off to him by Talbasta, to one day share with Helena Grace Hank.

"The land used to have a gulf, but not anymore, now it's an island, of course. The trunk in your care, was originally found by Queen Mar. She was in hiding from her dangerous brother who kept invading people's homes and taking their valuables. He was a prince, meant to be King, and his name was Pale. Mar's husband King Alejandro killed Pale without ease, and Pale had a following of people that acted as he did. They called themselves pirates, and they would march in his honor.

Rill was Alejandro and Mar's son, the crowned prince, and he decided to live in the cave surrounded by treasure. Meredith, Rill's sister, the second born took the throne of the island, and sponsored her sister the Princess Arcelia of Talley Gulf Island to go on adventures across the globe. She took two men with her, Mario and Perrin. Perrin was her fiancé..."

Talbasta would have continued, but Captain Hank stopped him. "I'm impressed that you remember this story with all those names." Captain Hank was trying his best to listen to his best friend's nephew.

"Well, I'll tell you the rest..." Talbasta continued not realizing that was Captain Hank's way of trying to get him to stop talking. "Princess Arcelia was the one who found more of the treasures. Perrin enjoyed the traveling, and would bring the treasures back to this island. The only one that we know from her discoveries is the water.

Queen Meredith knew the people much better than Princess Arcelia and only let the people use the treasure under conditions out of caution for thieves. Princess Arcelia did not approve, but Queen Meredith did not need it. Queen Meredith married Melchior and they had two boys, Lence and Adelio. Princess Arcelia and Perrin had eleven girls, five sets of twins after their first born whose name was Najwa. Rill and Suki had one girl, Naif Sachi.

There was a war on the island with invading pirates who wanted the treasure at the time and the first Lence died in the war. Queen Meredith felt she was being judged for the argument that erupted between her and Princess Arcelia. Naif Saki was heartbroken by her family and she never married. Adelio, Queen Meredith's other son, brought peace between the queen and her sister. Adelio named their first-born son Lence.

Lence became a very noble young prince and saved the kingdom from being overtaken with pirates at age eighteen. He vowed he would always keep the treasure safe. That same week he saved Princess Kalina Grace from across the sea, who was shipwrecked. That is how Prince Lence and Princess Grace met. They fell in love and tested the different treasures together." Talbasta stopped to breathe, and added, "Nobody really knows what they learned, but they created the royal map that is now lost.

It is clear in the law that the treasure must be taken by another Grace and Lence. I was given special permission as the child of a Grace and Lence to watch after it all this time. I know the lineage, but I wish I knew more about the treasure. I hope this information I do have helps you on your journey."

Captain Hank said his goodbyes with Talbasta and thanked him for the intel. He said to Talbasta. "You can call me Seth. It was nice to meet you, and I'll do my best to remember the story. Your father would want me to," He shook his hand.

Captain Seth Hank took his oath seriously, especially at the risk of his daughter. When Captain Hank exited the ship to retrieve Helena, it left the treasure in the ship vulnerable to the pirates who were tracking it. Soon enough, the ship was infiltrated by pirates, who slowly took over and began corrupting the passengers. However, the pirates never found the watery treasure hidden aboard the ship.

After recalling these events, Talbasta never made it back to his home.

83

CHAPTER 11

The sunset had already come and gone, leaving the night to reign in the sky. August would never admit he was worried, but he could sense worry and emotions returning. However, he suppressed them to regain his self-control. Weariness weighed heavily in his own eyes despite his efforts, as he felt Helena looking at him. He tried to avoid eye contact with her due to unsteady emotions. August could not determine what he might say or how he might act in the aftermath of the liquid.

"What do you think is going on out there?" Helena whispered. Her manner was still and comforting to August.

"I don't know," he stuttered.

"Are you worried?" Helena continued despite a jittery tone plaguing his voice.

"No," August answered. He was desperately pursuing silence, and shooting down all of Helena's attempts at conversing.

August had not discovered Helena's secret that she had figured out what the red eyes meant. When he saw her smirk, his heart skipped a beat, it was as if Helena knew that he was lying. She met his fatigue with another gentle question, "August, would you lie to me to make me feel safe?"

This time, he looked at her. "Yes," he replied authentically. When looking at her, he could see her eyes were glistening. Though she looked worn as he did, Helena did not appear afraid. He took her hand in his, as they sat on the clay floor, waiting.

A glimmer of light pierced through the circular opening in the roof of the attic where they were sitting together. They perceived it as a bright star, that could have easily been mistaken for a planet in the galaxies above. Moonlight began mixing in with the other light from the heavens. Toward the left side of the room something uncertain started shimmering in the light.

August tossed Helena's hand back onto her lap, as he shot up and chased after the reflection from the sky.

"Ouch!" August said, as he stubbed his foot on what appeared to be some sort of chest. The light streaming in from the opening in the attic intensified. "Yeah, I'm okay thanks for asking," he sarcastically stated. Helena sent him a scrutinizing glance, which he did not know how to interpret. August moved closer to her. "Do you think it's the treasure?"

Helena was silent.

On the outside of the treasure chest, it had an elf owl engraved on it, which were the most prominent animals on the island. The feet of the chest were crafted after the bird's talons.

The chest was completely sealed, but when the light of the moon reached it, a line along the edge of the silver chest and a crescent shape lock appeared. A singular moonbeam filled the space and unlocked the mystical box before them. On its own accord, the lid lifted and a bright radiant glow sprang out from within.

Piles of gold coins lay inside, identical to the coins that August had found in his pockets on the ship. Reaching into his pocket he pulled out a gold coin, and Helena picked up one of the coins from the chest to compare. August turned his face to Helena with wonder as the glowing gold reflected off their skin.

Helena's feelings were hurt earlier when August tossed her hand to the side when the treasure chest appeared. She glanced down at her hand and wiped it on her clothes. Her jaw was clenched before, but now she was willing to put her pride aside for their mission.

Noticing a small gold, button in the back of the inner lining of the chest, she pressed it. The coins that were sitting in a shallow, silver tray elevated slowly. An even brighter light began to shine. August was squinting his eyes to try to see it, but Helena's abilities allowed her to see clearly as she studied the contents further.

The elevated tray revealed an internal flame coming off what appeared to be a small plank of wood shaped like a heart. It looked so beautiful like a flaming diamond, but its brown color showed its true nature. The plank's flames beat swiftly like wings.

"I wonder what it does?" Reaching into the chest once more, Helena took hold of the flaming plank. August reached to stop her arm, but he hesitated.

The flame was real, but instead of burning it stung her hands like a hundred bees. She tossed it away, but towards August who instinctively caught it, burning his own hands as well. August screamed, as it stuck to his hands.

He shook violently as the plank fell from his hands. The seemingly, living plank flew back into the treasure chest from whence it came.

August watched in shock for a moment. Helena believed she caused this, and guilt entered her heart. Typically, her impulsive actions brought good fortune, but maybe that was null with the use of a treasure?

Helena mirrored August, as she looked to her hands. There were no burns, blisters, or pain. She looked down at August, who was still laying on the floor, and he gazed up at her. His expression seemed to speak to her, that they were going to experience different side effects than they had with the liquid. Similarly to taking the medicine, Helena dropped to the floor, next to August, and they both slipped into states of unconsciousness.

CHAPTER 12

Meanwhile, Avril was still alive. She was attempting to find her way to her brother. While he had been looking for her, she had been looking for him. Their paths never crossed, as Avril never went to the control room of the cruise ship.

Once Avril was off the ship, she was searching the pathway that she had taken with her parents on the island. She heard her name being called. "Avril!" The shaky voice said. Avril had rushed over, seeing a figure who looked like August, but this person was Talbasta. Talbasta had been attacked by pirates while protecting the pathway between his house and the ship, and he was dying.

As Talbasta faded, he said to Avril, "Avril, you may not remember me, but..." He trailed off, while handing her a cloth from his pocket. He wrapped his compass in it and placed it in Avril's hand. He shook his head, knowing he did not have time. "August and Helena are in my house. The clay one. It's twenty minutes from here if you follow the path."

Talbasta pointed to the handkerchief. The beginning of the prophecy he spent his life studying, was embroidered on it. It was his mother's. He hoped that it truly meant something. If not, it was nice knowing that his mother's possession was passed on, as he was passing on to the next stage of life - death. "Avril, *Half of the moon is taken by the footprints, the flower...*" He recited until his last breath exhaled from his body.

Avril could not help but cry, looking at the face of a man who looked so much like her brother.

It took nearly an hour for Avril to find the house, but she found where Talbasta had instructed her to go. She hurried inside. Eventually finding the winding, clay staircase, she made her way up the stairs.

The room was dark, but Avril could see the treasure chest on the side of the room. It was now shut, being that the moon had drifted along in the night's sky, but the box still shone. She was filled with curiosity and ran her fingers along the ornate box, not seeing Helena and August on the floor in the shadows of the room.

It had been six hours since Helena and August passed out from the effects of the burning heart treasure. Helena started waking up and the first thing she saw as her eyes opened, was Avril touching the box. Helena jolted up to stop Avril, not realizing that the trunk had been closed. Helena knocked Avril to the floor to keep her from getting burned.

"What was that for?" Avril demanded, and then immediately hugged Helena as she realized it was her. She insisted further, "What happened?"

"I thought you were about to..." Helena began to answer, but August piled on into a group hug with Avril.

Avril shrieked, cupping her brother's face in both her hands, "You're alive!" Then the three teens huddled together once more.

As they made their way downstairs, Avril heard Helena turn back. "My hairpin," the English girl muttered. August continued following Avril down the stairs, asking if there was a man anywhere near the house. Avril relayed what happened to the man who gave her the handkerchief.

After a few minutes of silence, Avril added, "August, he somehow knew me. He said that we had met before. He gave me this handkerchief."

August took it, as Avril watched him read. He reached into his pocket and pulled out a coin. "Do you see this etching?"

"Barely," she scoffed.

"It has the same wording on it," August stated.

"It also has the same elf owl on the front of it like that trunk in the attic," Avril added. She did not realize that she was not supposed to be able to see the treasure chest. Avril was not a Lence or a Grace.

"Avril, how come you could see the treasure and how did you escape the pirates?" August asked her. Avril was at a loss for words.

When Avril and August had first started down the stairs, and Helena went back for her hairpin, three pirates descended into the home from the opening in the roof. One of the pirates covered Helena's mouth, and the others hoisted the pirate back out of the attic as he held onto her. The pirates were unable to see the treasure, right under their noses.

On the roof, one of the pirates introduced himself to Helena. "Hello there, I'm Ammon, and I'm your new best friend." He did not tie her hands or duct tape her mouth, though he had the supplies close by as an intimidation tactic. That was clearly a last resort, as he was hoping for things to go the easy way and not the hard way. He stuck a pen in her right hand and a piece of paper in her left.

Helena threw it on the floor, unwilling to even begin to write, whatever they were expecting her to divulge. Plus, Helena was left-handed when she wrote. They forced the pen and paper back into her hand.

"Here is the deal, Sunshine, you are gonna answer all of our questions and we won't kill your little friend Talbasta." His sense of seriousness was burrowed into the lines in his skin, while his resting face harbored an expression that resembled a smile. He almost looked like her own father in this way. His temperament was very cool, but when Helena threw the pen and paper on the floor again, he acted. "Pick it up."

She did not. Ammon looked down with a ponderous look, and picked up the pen and placed it in her left hand and the paper in her right. He blocked her from throwing it. "Don't throw it again. It's a nice pen. Use it – don't use it, but don't abuse it. The pen and paper are here so you can communicate with duct tape over your mouth. I'm letting you hold it as a courtesy, and I'm allowing you to speak as a courtesy. You're gonna answer the questions one way or another."

"I'll only answer one for you to give us back Talbasta. Then let me go," Helena pleaded.

He laughed melodiously. "Okay, but he won't do very well without his limbs I'm afraid." Helena's eyes watered and he put up his sleeve to dry her eyes, but she turned her head away.

Avril, who was still in the kitchen with August, did not answer his questions. "Bro, if you're really quiet you can hear gunshots. I think this island has a real pirate problem," Avril observed cautiously.

"That sounds more like a helicopter," August argued back.

"Captain Hank was telling the passengers to leave all their jewelry and stuff on the boat while you and your little girlfriend were getting fried together. How romantic, by the way," she joked.

"She isn't my girlfriend, Avril. I think we might like each other though..." August mumbled as he uncomfortably shifted, looking younger for the first time since he had the treasure water.

"Well, let me ask you a question, why isn't your non-girlfriend back down here yet?" She asked.

"Probably to get away from you. I don't know. She said she was looking for something," he responded uneasily to his sister.

"You should go make sure she is okay," said the teasing, but serious, Avril Bridges to her little brother.

"I think you should tell me how you got away from the pirates, survived the battle, and could see the treasure. Now Talbasta is dead and you're the last one to see him alive. How?" August responded.

A helicopter was hovering above Talbasta's roof. August had dashed up the stairs to the clay attic to see the whirling propellers. Panicking, he shouted, "Helena? Helena!" He skipped steps as he got up to the top. She was gone.

Helena could hear August calling for her. It was enough to almost make her cry, but a thought occurred to her instead. She remembered him tossing her hand aside to look at the Talley Gulf Treasure. *Now* he noticed her absence. Her anger took over, and she did not fight the pirates as she climbed into the helicopter with them before August could see her. She glanced at the house below, but with a clenched jaw she turned and looked ahead, as she hardened her heart. She flew away with the pirates, in attempts that it would save Talbasta who she did not know was already dead.

Disconcerted, August did not know what to do, as he could not get onto the roof. He saw the helicopter low in the sky and he screamed, "No! Bring her back. Don't take Helena. Take me! I love her!"

The pirates heard nothing, but Helena heard August's distant words. She leaned over to look out the window and she could see August through the opening in the attic. She reached toward the window with her knotted hands. Despite August's emotionless behavior, Helena knew he was still in there, and she wanted to see him again. She regretted her brash action, and had to trust that the luck in her anger would persevere.

Her face lifted, and across from her sat a pirate who had bands across his forearms, but no higher. It must have been a trick of the light because for a moment, she thought he seemed sympathetic. He had blonde hair that was a warmer tone than her own, crystal blue eyes, and sun kissed skin. The stranger averted her gaze and looked out the window. Helena noticed the weapon he held tightly. One of the bands on his wrist seemed to be covering a tattoo. The edge of the ink almost looked like the edge of the symbol on the back of the coin August had given her. With her hands tied, she could not reach into her pocket. Nor was this pirate going to let her move one of his bands for comparison. Curiosity beamed from her eyes.

He looked back at her and snapped, "Do you mind? Stop staring." He gestured with his weapon in the direction she should look.

Helena gulped nervously at the weapon, but looked directly into his eyes in defiance. Silently they were locked in an unspoken competition until her opponent rolled his eyes and looked out the window. Helena mirrored his action as the helicopter neared the shore of the island, and she wondered what was going to happen to her now.

Back at the house, Avril came running when she heard a painful scream coming from above her. She stormed in only to see August jumping to try to reach the roof. "They took her, and I screamed at the top of my lungs that I loved her. I can't believe I did that. I know she heard me. They've got her, and they're gonna use what I said against her. This is not good." He stopped, gazing at the opening in the attic.

"August, she is smart," Avril advised. "She'll be okay, and we'll get her back. Let's try to find Captain Hank." Avril pulled him.

"Avril," August started as they left Talbasta's house. "I should not have said that I loved Helena in that way, but I do love her – in a way. After I had that healing water, I could not feel anything, and she is the only one who could make me feel – so that must mean something, right? I think I might love her, in my head I think I do, but I still feel a little numb. Like my emotions are there, but they all hurt."

Avril listened. She wanted to make some kind of joke, but she refrained. Suddenly, August screamed in pain, dropping to his knees in front of her. The burns from the treasure were not visible, but tortured August nonetheless.

Once the helicopter landed, Helena was taken to a small boat, and the boat returned to the cruise ship. Helena's invisible injury began to burn once more. The pirates did not notice her struggle as they snuck her aboard. They thought that she was fighting them and not the pain. They brought her to a regular room with a balcony, and had her sit down in a chair.

Ammon, the pirate captain, said to Helena, "Time for answers, Sunshine, otherwise we'll tie you to Talbasta and drop you both into the depths of the ocean. Tell me where the treasures are."

Helena tried to use the pen she was given, but the instrument started boiling. It melted and spilled the hot ink all over the paper and the floor. Ammon looked at her in disbelief.

Ammon gestured for his second in command to take over. This was the pirate who had sat across from her in the helicopter. He was no longer covered in tactical gear, and she could see his mix of pirate garb and modern beach attire. He was the most handsome person Helena had ever seen, which made her nervous that he was now in charge. He did not look like he belonged with the enemy, and for the second in command, he did not seem to care for Ammon. Helena wanted to figure out why.

The pirate captain left to continue the search for treasure, leaving his top lead - to his partner. Ammon was not going to waste his own time, as they were not getting much from Helena regardless of her being their best lead. The second in command sent the other, lower ranking pirates away.

The second in command was now alone with Helena. He stepped up very close to her. Once the man heard no sounds, he whispered, "I'm not your enemy, Helena Grace Hank, those men think I am my identical twin brother Mark. Mark was a pirate, and I am not a pirate." He met her gaze, as he began to untie her. "It has not been easy. A lot of these pirates were born into it. They have a lot of rules about adopting the piracy lifestyle. It mainly involves people getting killed. I'm sure you know that – you seem quite capable." He glanced at the dissolved pen and ink on the floor, "However, you need protection, and I'm here to serve you, Grace." He bowed his head. "Lexus Corazana, at your service.

"Did you know Talbasta?" Helena asked him, as he called her by her full name and performed the same slight bow as Talbasta. "How do I know I can trust you?"

He answered, "This is how." He pulled a flaming wood heart out of his pocket. He held it in his hands, and it did not burn him.

"Why isn't it burning you?" She asked him in amazement.

"Two reasons..." He said placing it in her hands, which scared her but did not burn her this time. "They grow on the island. This is only the third one to be found in existence. You've already been stung by one, so you can't be stung again."

"Stung?" She questioned in confusion.

"Yes," he replied. "It's a living plant. It won't burn those who are in love. It can sense a person who has emotional instability and it attaches itself to the human its honed in on. Then the plant syncs up with a person's heart rate by feeling the pulse as it stings them." This informative explanation allowed Helena to relax while holding the creature. "It gives you clarity of what you want. The flame continues to burn because there are always more people who are not in love or don't know what they want. It reaches out like a vine to find them, and feeds off that energy. If it was placed on the ground it would roll like a tumble weed. However, the royals put a magnetic mechanism on them to keep them in treasure troves. This one was free range from the main tree of the island."

He asked Helena, interrupting her smiling down on the unusual lifeform. "So, which one are you?"

"What do you mean?" she asked.

"Are you in love? If so – who with?" The young man asked Helena bluntly. She looked at him without answering. He raised an eyebrow as if he understood that it was complicated. He then guided her back off the ship in silence. They took a small vessel to shore. Eventually reaching a short, stone stairway dug into the beach that led to bronze double doors in the ground.

"Wait," she said. "Will I be safe if I walk down those steps."

"Yes." He spoke.

"So, you're not gonna hurt, kill, or lie to me or the people I love?" Her eyes narrowed, looking for a sign of deception.

"No," he chuckled. "Look, I understand if you don't want to believe me, but I'm a direct descendant of past royals of Talley Gulf Island. The ones that no one talks about," he clarified.

"You're a royal?" Helena examined his eyes once again as he answered, the absence of crimson rings confirmed that he was telling her the truth.

"Yes, but there isn't a throne for me or any of the other descendants anymore. The protectors were given charge of the Island instead." The young man said while kicking a small rock in the sand before he began descending the first step. He turned to her, offering her his hand. Helena took his hand, and he helped her down the stairs. Quietly, he continued speaking to her. "I'm part of the Page Society." The door opened to reveal an underground tunnel, with low ceilings. It was like a house of mirrors. The mirrors were placed throughout the tunnel to spread the source of light from a different flaming heart plant. Helena had never seen such a thing, as it looked like there were hundreds of fires around them.

"Woah," she commented. She heard people talking loudly in the distance. The sound was coming from deeper in the tunnel, and she instinctively stepped forward to go further. Helena felt Lexus's hand gently press her arm as he stopped her from continuing.

"I brought you down here so we could talk freely, but you cannot proceed. You're not a member. It's a society of a secretive nature. You can only know it exists because you're a Grace, but you're not a Page or a royal." He gestured toward himself. "We monitor the Island, and vast lands beyond the seas, but you didn't hear that from me. I'm a descendant, which is why I can see some of the treasures. Only descendants and royals can actually see it. It's because our ancestors were affected by the treasures so it's in our blood." He smirked. "Anyway, I can tell you're not interested in all that... you want to know who I'm in love with because it doesn't burn me." He gleamed, twirling a piece of her hair that came loose, from where she had repinned it.

"You want to talk?" She asked him.

"Yes, I love to talk. It's my fatal flaw, so I've been told. There was once a girl, she was a beautiful girl, on this boat during the Pirates versus Passengers War. She was stuck in a burning room with a bunch of other people and I showed her a way out. I saved her life. I thought to myself – I'll never see that girl again, but I remembered how I felt when I saw her leave. My heart went with her, even though I could not." He explained.

"I wonder if I knew her?" Helena said brightly.

Lexus's eyes twinkled, but he shook out of his glee with a nonchalant tone. "You might of, but it doesn't matter now. I'll die someday. Maybe not now, but I will die. Acting as a pirate is too dangerous, but first I have to keep you safe." He walked over to the wall, and set the second heart down by the mirrors, and the place doubled in light. He smiled widely. "I may not be great at flying a helicopter, but I can navigate," he told Helena in regards to the treasure. "I can get you back to that house."

"We should take Talbasta back with us?" Helena suggested, following Lexus as he turned toward a room.

"No. You may want to cover your eyes and ears."

"Why?" She questioned crossly.

"Um, he is dead, and when I open this door – you'll see his body." He flexed his hands before opening the door, and pulling out the corpse of Talbasta. Helena was absolutely mortified.

Lexus stated, "Here is the plan. You hide down here, while I place Talbasta in the water out there." Helena's expression of disgust led Lexus to add further explanation, "I promise it's above board. He's gonna be our distraction, as I set off the alarms for the pirates. Talbasta was one of us, so he was taken back here. It is part of his oath to help living or dead. If any pirates stop us, I'm going to tell them it was you who killed him. They would then think you're one of them now, a pirate. After that I'll join you. Is it a bad plan? Yes, but it is a plan, so stay put."

Helena gave a slight smirk despite her newly enacted trauma. She could not help but wonder if she would ever have a crush on a normal guy? It was useless for her to pretend Lexus's beauty had not mesmerized her mind. The way that August had tossed her hand had not departed from her senses.

The question, "Think that'll work?" came from the doorway, as one of the pirates Lexus had sent away, followed them here and opened the door to the secret society. He held a knife up to Lexus.

Lexus had a melodious laugh as if he did not see the pirate as a threat. He mockingly said, "Well, I won't cower if that's what you're thinking." He elbowed the pirate in the gut, grabbing the knife and turned it on the pirate. "I thought I told you earlier to get away from me, and you disobeyed. Do you know what happens to disobedient pirates." They both knew the answer, as Lexus took the small glass vile out of his pocket. The pirate shook his head, grabbing the knife back from Lexus. Lexus's arm caught on the blade and it sliced through his leather outerwear.

Helena threw up her hands in annoyance turning toward the tunnel, examining the hallway as she wondered if anyone was hearing this commotion. She turned back to face them, and they dropped the knife and she took it from their grasps. Lexus got the pirate to the ground after he snatched the vile from his hand.

Lexus punched him with enough force to render the enemy unconscious. He dragged the enemy to the other members in the secret society. Lexus could not let this person go back into the world with the knowledge of the society. They would have to try to rehabilitate his mind and body.

Helena's hand was bleeding from the pirate trying to take the knife back from her. Lexus seemed to be fine, but he had dislocated his right shoulder when he punched the pirate hard enough to knock him out.

Once Lexus got rid of the pirate, he said to Helena, "Come with me, I need your help stitching this cut." He was speaking her language, and then with his uninjured arm he took her hand in his.

With a blush she said, "If there are more pirates tracking either of us, they could find us here in this place – like he did."

"Helena, do you know what the healing treasure is?" He asked her in the first serious tone he had truly used, adding, "Because if you know where it is – you can tell me, and I'll go get it for you if you want to hide down here with that knife. Then we can head to Talbasta's place... or you could come with me – we would just need to be careful. Your choice, which will it be?"

Helena was surprised he gave her a choice instead of just barking orders at her thinking he knew best. From the corner of her eye, realizing if she did not go with him, either of them might end up being killed like Talbasta. They would be safer together. "I'm going with you," she answered decidedly, not wanting to be alone again.

He nodded in agreement, but still asked her once more, "Are you sure?"

"I'm pretty sure. You know this tunnel inside and out. I know the ship inside and out. With our combined knowledge of secret tunnels – and what not – I'm sure. If I stayed here something bad could happen to you and I'd be alone again. I don't want that – I've done that before on the ship. I'd be there alone not knowing if it was a solitude that was lasting or temporary. I don't want to go through that again. Plus, I'm pretty sure we are wasting precious time talking about it," she answered handing him the bloody knife in bold confidence.

They stepped out into the wind above ground. Helena noticed a yearning glance from Lexus, as the wind pushed her hair from her eyes. She may have looked strong and mysterious, but she felt vulnerable. He had the knife in his hand, he was forging their path despite his injury, but she was following his lead. His steady stare waned into a smile. In his eyes, she could see a twinge of sadness and sympathy. Helena pulled the bottle out of her pocket, knowing it to be the mysterious liquid she and August had before. "Take a sip," she instructed him. He thought it was regular water, and took a sip of the elixir, with no warning of the coming side effects.

CHAPTER 13

Back at Talbasta's house, August was staring at the doorway with a knot in his throat, hoping Helena would walk through the opening. Avril made him some tea, as he sat down in a chair, shaking. He felt like he had when he was hiding in the cabinet on the ship. Some of the tea sloshed out of the blue mug he was holding loosely. It landed on his gold producing slacks.

"You okay? You haven't said a word since you told Captain Hank about Helena. August, you need to speak. It's rude to ignore people who are trying to be nice to you. Especially – when it's your caring sister," Avril said gently to her distraught brother.

He looked at her and all that could be seen in his eyes was regret, pain, sorrow, and a numb spirit. He took a deep breath and spoke ten words, "I should have never let her out of my sight."

"August, it wasn't your fault —" Avril spoke, but was interrupted.

"Well, that's not what Captain Hank said," August stated.

"I don't care, August, it doesn't matter what he said or what he thinks. It was not your fault," Avril demanded, but he would not hear it.

"I was supposed to keep her safe, Avril, it was my fault. It is," August admitted, while Avril shook her head. "It was, Avril. This whole trip has been my fault. Remember? I was the one who suggested we take a cruise in the first place because of that book I read. Then I got us kicked off this island, when Mom and Dad detoured our trip and wanted to come here. Then I got dragged into a room by Helena's father who was waiting for me to show up. It all leads back to me," he protested. Avril and August sat in silence, with the embers crackling beside them from the fireplace. There was no more celebration, nor was there war, there was only quiet.

August knew that his sister was not a person who enjoyed silence. Avril asked positively, "You are one of the most selfless people I know, so I find this situation ironic. Wanna know why?"

"No, but get to your point," he appealed.

She nudged him for his shortage of enthusiasm. "Look, why are you having regrets? Think of the people's lives that you helped save."

"Avril, don't. Don't you get it? Helena is gone. None of any of that other stuff matters. I may have saved some other people, but I didn't save Mom or Dad – and now we lost Helena, too." August raved. "And I didn't save you; I am just lucky you're alive."

"I miss them, too, August. They were my parents and Helena was my friend, too! That's what I don't get right now..." Avril said.

"Don't get what?" He sighed.

"You acting like this. All I'm hearing you say – is – you – you – you – all about you. The fact is, if we never went on this trip *your* Helena could be dead or still trapped. Do you understand that? You did as much as you could or at least pushed them in the right direction. If you love Helena Hank so much – why are you regretting meeting her and saving her life? You made her life better too, August, and for all we know, she could be just fine. You know that girl is like a ninja. Mom and dad were being controlled somehow. I know it, I could see it in their eyes. It was like the other adults." Avril articulated her point.

August listened, but did not react. Avril began putting the fire out. August had been concentrating, but welcomed the interruption from his stare. "Do you think Captain Hank reached the ship, yet?" August questioned his sister.

"Yes, probably," she answered. August turned his head from the dark fireplace to the light gleaming in from the entryway. He sustained his stare out into the world.

In a rowboat far out into the water sat Helena and Lexus trying to row as quickly as they could. They were coping with exhaustion. They had been rowing away from rogue pirates all night after trying to use Talbasta's corpse as a diversion in the water. They wished they had tried their plan a little differently. Helena would have been happy to have pretended to still be a prisoner, but Lexus was seen fighting other pirates. Hence their current predicament.

"Watch out!" Helena tried to warn Lexus of an unknown entity sticking out of the water. It hit their boat.

"Sorry," Lexus said in an exhausted tone, as he looked out to try and see what it was. It was a large stone pointed out of the water. It was a treasure chest made of stone that was adhered to the point. "Helena, look. It's one of the treasures. Go and get it!" He suggested.

"You go get it! Actually... I don't think we can take the whole thing back with us, it's a rock – we'd sink," Helena debated. "We'll just have to try to find it again. Neither of us can reach it anyway."

They knew they most likely would not find this place again once they left. Lexus was babbling, but all Helena kept hearing Lexus muttering something about *twelve days* under his breath. They were sun stroked, hungry, and sleep deprived. They needed to get back to the island.

"Shut up, and look!" Helena took his arm and pointed behind him. She'd been focused on the highest part they could see on Talley Gulf Island. "You can see the top of the mountain from exactly this point. You can tell which side of the island we're on, too." She looked at Lexus with a smirk and said, "We can find it again someday - let's row back."

"Melva," he said, which caused a furrow in Helenas brow.

"What?" Helena asked.

"Melva. She was a princess born at the same time the treasure was discovered. In that box is the rock armor that only one of the protectors can wear. They don't know how it was forged – it's supposedly ancient, but it adjusts to fit whoever wears it. It's very cool," he explained to Helena, much like a professor.

The rest of Lexus and Helena's journey would be mostly quiet. Lexus's soothing voice failed to provide the passion or excitement the way it had on land. Helena missed the saturation and depth of his voice. She wondered if the elixir had the opposite effect on Lexus? Maybe he was too perfect to possibly improve or she was too tired to appreciate his improvements?

Eventually, they finally crawled onto the beach, soaking wet. When they arrived, the sun had set, and in the dark they could hear marching. Lexus stood, dodging their swords, darts, and vials. Helena unsheathed her tiny dagger that doubled as her hairpin. However, her action triggered a memory. She recalled the battle on board the cruise ship and how August had placed a coin in each of his parent's hands. Helena took the coin that August had given her, out of her pocket, and opened the coin like she had done once before. Exposing the powder on the inside of the coin, Helena took a deep breath and blew the dust at their foes. When the dust reached the pirate's skin, a few of them vanished. In seeing this, the others ran.

Lexus and Helena grabbed onto each other's hands and found a spot to hide. They curled up together and rested. Helena's head placed on his chest; she fell quickly asleep in his arms. Lexus held her, placing his brother's pirate cape over her to shield her from sight, while he remained uncovered to face any foes that might approach. Aside from his exhaustion, he was content.

CHAPTER 14

While Avril slept peacefully, August decided to take a walk. Breathing in the beach air felt like a healing elixir for August's broken soul.

The white sand moved from beneath August's slowly traveling feet. He did not get very far before he stumbled upon a house. It was a well taken care of home with a lovely lawn. This home was clearly occupied. His stomach rumbled, alerting him of his need for food. The carefree, and now truly adventurous boy, opened the picket fence outlining the property and entered hoping to encounter hospitality. With heavy feet and heavier eyelids, his heart led him to the pathway to the front of the house. He knocked more than once, and the door unlocked and swayed open.

"Finally!" A man with a drink in his hand asked in an irate manner. "Are you August? Come in and make it snappy."

August entered with unease. "How do you know me?" Expressed concern ventured from the boy's lips.

"Don't act so nervous. Everyone on the good side knows the name Lence, and anyone could tell by your burns if they can see the treasures. Those burns are clear signs that you're not ordinary at all, but you're a leader, a prince, and a Page!" August heard. It swiftly altered his attention to the words this man was speaking and away from food and sleep.

"A Page?" Questioned the boy, now squinting in confusion.

"Protector. Don't act stupid. The Society! The Pages! The Protectors. You know what you need to do. Get it done. My whole family died one night – just because I left to get a cake for my daughter's birthday. I'm assuming that now ya wanna know why?" said the man aggressively. "Because I had two of the treasure chests in my house. I was keeping them for Talbasta. I promised I'd find someone to get them off of the island, but then I figured who could be safer than me? Pirates can't stay on the island long with a Grace and

Lence here. With the protector's being gone for so long the pirates have all but taken over, but they only pillage at night. With you and the Grace here the treasure is safe."

August began to realize he and Helena could see the treasure more easily at night from the liquid's effect on their eyes. That was when they needed to protect it. Their heightened abilities helped them protect the treasures and people from the horrendous pirates.

"Helena isn't here though; the pirates kidnapped her right before the break of dawn. I knew there must have been a reason they didn't go back for the treasure," spilled the disturbed boy.

"Why did you let her get kidnapped? That's stupid. You and I could die at any moment if she isn't on the island with you. We only got one day of peace because of you! Take the treasures and get out of my house. Good luck to ya. You're gonna need it!" He shouted tossing the boy the heavy yet small treasure chests outside of the man's house. All he wanted was food and sleep, and all he got was more responsibility.

A gold coin fell lightly out from the inside of August's pocket to the man's feet. The man cautiously picked it up and uttered, "Never in my life have I ever thought I'd see one of these – judging – me. I'm not like you – one day you'll understand." He burst into dust in front of August's eyes. August stood completely still, his eyes wide, and his jaw dropped. The recent trauma that August had been exposed to had been too much for his newly revitalized emotions to comprehend. He attempted to process the shock that he had endured.

August heard the rustling of bushes, and was convinced he was about to be attacked.

Instead, Avril came out from behind them. "Bro, are those tiny treasure chests?" She asked. Curiosity ran in the Bridges family. Without answering her, he gestured for her to carry one.

August walked with Avril back to the beach. They then decided to open the treasure chests together. Avril did not ask what her brother's reasoning was for waiting until they got to the shore, nor did she ask what his next move would be. She waited for him to be ready to tell her. "I need to get whatever is inside the treasure chests and put it in my backpack." He spoke with a tone she had not heard him use in a while; it had the same tone of familial love, but with a twinge of pain.

He opened the chest that had blue stones on it. Much like the flaming wooden heart box, it also had a button and a rising tray inside.

Avril watched how carefully August opened the box. They observed a gold tray lifting and revealing what was underneath. Such beauty arose from under the tray in the form of an elegant fan. It must have been made with satin and gold. Avril decided to pick it up and fan the air. August took it from her and did the same.

August was unaware that every time he and Helena came in contact with one of Talley Gulf treasures, a sway of peace and protection would ripple over the land. August placed the fan back into the box. A feeling of peace took the place of August's depression. This was what the Talley Gulf Island natives called the Peace Fan. It was a symbol on their currency.

August opened the next box. Once the small, heavy trunk had been opened, a wave of memories flooded his mind. They were memories of Helena which lightened up his world and after the cloud lifted there was a single ring that lay in the box. The colors on it were simple but captivating. The ring was a cranberry red with a silver line completely encompassing its center. The silver line had rippling ridges in it around the circumference.

August took the ring in his hands. That ring felt as if he had a deep connection to it when he noticed the engraving on the band that read, *"Grace et Lence aeternitas."* August blinked, holding it as if it were a star fallen from the sky directly into his hands.

It must have been Talabasta's parents' rings and the Grace and Lence before them. Generations of partners that took care of the Talley Gulf treasure and the citizens of the island had worn this ring. August equipped his ring finger with the charming band and he knew what it meant to those who had gone before him. August felt like himself again for the first time since he drank the mysterious liquid. There was a part of him that was restored when he waws with Helena, but this treasure returned his emotions completely. There was no humming, buzzing, or feeling one emotion at a time. He now had the full range of his emotions. This gave him hope. He was surprised there were not two of them, but he would bring this ring to Helena and give it to her when he found her. He smiled for the first time since he lost her.

August turned to Avril. "Let's go find Helena," he stated sternly.

Avril never wanted to step foot on the ship again after her experience being taken by the pirates and she was not one to keep secrets. "August, I don't wanna go back. Why don't I stay here on the island and see if Helena comes here. I can look for more of the treasures and keep the boxes nice and safe for you guys to open." Her voice quivered as she explained, with a great deal of anxious gesturing.

"I would prefer you stay with me," August responded.

"Then don't go," Avril pleaded.

"I hate to, but I have to," he stated with a kind but determined voice.

"Why?" She questioned.

"Just come with me. I was supposed to protect Helena and stay with her, but I didn't and now – she might be dead. I don't want that to be the case when it comes to you. You're my sister. I love you. Stay with me, so I can keep you safe." Tears formed in August's eyes and his voice quaked as he held back his emotions. They were finally having the honest conversation they needed to have after all their pain.

Avril stared for a moment, but her blank expression transformed like a light switched on and she smiled. Placing her hand on August's shoulder she said, "Then – I'm going with you." Her profile lessened in its brightness after her brother grinned because of the reality of what her words meant. She leaned closer to her little brother who was now much taller than her and she said, "I'm your big sister, and you still need to listen to me because not only do I have that position – and intuition." She took a pause with clenched teeth, serious eyes, and said something that was unexpected for her, "I'm not gonna let you die alone."

He tried pulling away and brushing off her comment, but she was insistent. "Call it what you want, August, heartbreak, loss, post-traumatic stress, but I know if you go to the ship there is a good chance you won't be coming back for me and then I won't have anyone. You and I both know, we did not rid the ship of the pirates. They will probably – well I don't want to say it."

August was deeply troubled by her words after being so filled with hope. He replied, "I'm gonna take a quick nap first, okay?"

S he nodded and sat there thinking about every word she told him when she noticed the skyline above the ocean was not straight. A waft drifted into the air around August as he slept, that woke him up right after he drifted off to sleep. "Do you smell that?" He spoke. He pointed to where the smell seemed to be coming from as he sat up. It was coming from the same direction and point that Avril had noticed on the skyline.

"You scared me, I thought you were sleeping," Avril gasped, clutching her chest. August laughed. The two siblings gathered the treasures they had with them, and were ready to continue their determined trek.

He answered, "That spot out there, where the scent and visual distortion is coming from, will need to be our first stop. Guess we aren't going to the ship right now – after all." Avril smiled.

They ventured to Talbasta's dark purple boat, and after many strokes in the ocean, they finally reached their destination point. The speck they had seen from so far away turned out to be a very large rock sticking out of the ocean. It was narrow and reached out into the air, but had a thick bottom portion, and a flat top section. Sitting high above their seats sat a silver box, was a treasure chest.

Avril climbed up the slippery, stone form and took the case carefully down. August helped her open it, but as Avril was taking point on this one, he was peering over her shoulder to see what was inside. This was the most prized possession of the royals on the island – the clarity crown.

It was lined with vertically set diamonds the size of the head of a pin. The rows were each four and a half inches tall. All the diamonds were set with silver and the band that would go across one's head was silver, as well.

Avril reached for the crown, but August knocked her hand away. "Don't touch it! You don't know what will happen if you do. These treasures throw you for a loop every time." They both analyzed it, carefully wrapped it up in Avril's plaid button up, and put it in August's backpack.

CHAPTER 15

A few days passed as August and Avril searched for Helena. Captain Hank had joined them. They were simultaneously searching for parts of the Talley Gulf Treasure. Now the three of them collectively held the Peace Fan, Reality Ring, Clarity Crown, as well as of portion of the liquid that Captain Hank still carried with him from the ship. They had harbored a few more possible treasures on their trek, but were thinking that they might be diversions for the pirates. They did not find it worth the risk to test any gifts these items might possess. They had found a pen, leaf, and fruit that glowed bright yellow. It was worth adding to their collection, if not worth the risk of using.

August had climbed to the top of one of the Talley Gulf Island's mountains that the map showed harbored one of the treasures. One of Talbasta's contacts had taken care of one of the treasures for him for a long time. At the peak, he found a glowing yellow rock, nearby to a withered skeleton. This must have been Talbasta's friend. August slowly picked up the glowing treasure, that was hidden under the dirt. August wondered why Talbasta's contacts were so loyal and never left the island. He reflected on his fate. The position of taking care of the treasures was dangerous. August took a deep breath and began his descent. When he reached the bottom, he walked to Captain Hank, but he tripped and fell over a hump in the soil.

August dug to find what could be there, and that was where he found a large, thickly layered papyrus. When he looked at it closely, he realized what it was – a treasure map! Not just to one treasure, but it displayed a list of locations to the other treasures. The question remaining was if they had successfully been placed in their hidden destinations or if they had been moved. Some were in an eligible script and different language, it listed what the treasures properties were, and was signed by a *Page VIII*. The only assumption to be made was that this was the royal map.

August looked at the other treasure he had in his hand. Captain Hank approached him, examining the piece of papyrus in August's hand, to see what the treasure could do in accordance with the map.

Captain Hank translated for them, *"Starlight wishing stone, allows you to wish for any object or person to be present with you, something you may need in the future will be with you, too."*

August looked at Captain Hank, knowing they would share the same wish of wanting to find Helena. A rustling came from the bushes behind them, and they turned with anticipation. Lexus and Helena walked out into the opening. August dropped the map and the treasure he was holding and ran to Helena. He pulled her onto her toes in the biggest bear hug to ever be given to another human. Lexus had to jump out of the way to not be trampled.

"Helena! I never thought I'd see you again." He kissed her on the cheek a few times out of pure glee. "I have missed you more than anyone in my entire life."

What they did not know was that a protective presence began radiating over the island because the future Grace and Lence were together again.

Helena pulled away, a rosy smile forming on her face. "We've walked so many miles, we just decided to go this way to rest..." Helena explained, and realized that August was attentively listening to her speak. A vast difference between now and him dropping her hand in Talbasta's clay attic.

Helena could immediately tell that August's full range of emotions had returned, and wanted to know how. She knew well enough to know both Avril and August were wanting to tell her everything that they had learned and were simply holding back.

"Where did you get that page and why is it on the ground?" Lexus interrupted, yanking the map from the dirt. "Shameful," he grumbled, glaring at August and Helena as they interacted.

"I'm August," August introduced himself confidently to the random guy Helena was with, holding out his hand to shake Lexus's. Interpreting the stranger's reaction as disappointment regarding the way he had handled the artifacts.

"I know, and I really don't care." Lexus grinned as August did not have time to react because Helena jumped in for another hug with August. Lexus took the map, and he placed it in Helena's bag as she was busy catching up with her loved ones. He then made his way toward a log and took a seat.

Helena said firmly, "I missed you." August felt Helena's hair on his face, and he gently stroked the soft locks.

He whispered, knowing she could hear him, "I love you." He nervously smiled at her. August was weary of the fact he once again blurted out that he loved Helena. This time it was in the first five minutes of him seeing her again, though he did excuse it as he was quite relieved that she was alive.

Helena then hugged her father. Captain Hank was beside himself with happiness. This was the second time his daughter was presumed dead and had turned up once more. He did not have hope that she was alive, and thought he was simply looking for her remains, but here she was in the flesh.

Captain Hank apologized for giving August such a hard time when Helena was taken, even though he did blame August and they both knew it. August blamed himself, so it was not a sore spot between the two of them.

After a while, Lexus sat next to Helena once they had built a fire. "Why didn't you tell him that you love him?" Lexus asked Helena. "This entire time, all you did was talk about him."

Helena jokingly mocked Lexus, "Only because it was a way to divert the conversation from you rambling on about the treasures and the island and the duties – plants and so on." Her smile brightened. Then realized he was being serious, and so she gave him her best answer, "Why do I do the things I do? Good question, but I don't have an answer for you."

"I go after love, and if you love someone – you should do the same," Lexus advised. "The Lence and Grace are always meant to be together. The eternal partners..." Lexus explained.

"Again, with the history lessons." Helena would not let him finish, and tried to make him laugh. "Where's the fun in that?" Helena kissed his cheek.

Avril was behind them with the firewood she had been collecting. She interrupted, "Excuse me, but this is our fire – HELENA HANK!" Avril squealed, dropping her collection. The two squealed and hugged.

Lexus immediately recognized Avril from the ship – he tucked his head down. He realized that perhaps Helena was right about him, and maybe he knew too much for his own good.

"Hi, I'm Avril," Avril leaned her head down to acknowledge Lexus.

He stood up and introduced himself to Avril. "Hi, I'm Lexus. We've met before..." He trailed off awkwardly. He seemed to only be suave when he spoke to Helena.

"I'm sorry I don't remember." She kindly and truthfully replied.

"I was the pirate that helped you escape," Lexus quietly explained.

Helena and Lexus began telling Avril about the treasure they had found. The rock armor and the expanding glass circle.

August watched Helena reunite with Avril from the corner of his eye. He was content and happy aside from being partly rattled.

"As far as I can tell, it looks like you're only missing one of the treasures – at least from the known listings," Captain Hank said to August as he observed the map that he retrieved from his daughter's bag.

"Do you think Lexus talks too much?" August asked Captain Hank, as he watched Lexus with Helena.

"I'm not saying anything about that," Captain Hank answered, but then he did put down the map quickly answering him in a hushed voice. "I'm almost positive that boy told my daughter about the rules of the flaming wood heart treasure," he stated and August turned his attention back to the captain. "That means, I'm almost certain, she already knew you were in love with her before you told her." August was not expecting his involvement of Captain Hank's opinion to backfire onto himself.

"How did you know about – that I told her that?" August asked the girl's father nervously.

"I'm very observant," the captain answered, looking back at the map, but then added, "I just want you to note that she was very troubled by that heart because it did not tell her she was in love. Now if you'll excuse me, I'm going to fix some food, since no one cares to read the royal map – that people have literally been looking for - for decades..." Captain Hank dwindled with an irritated grumble, handing August the map, as he stood and walked in the direction of the nearby market.

August re-joined the other teenagers, suggesting they put the treasures away because it was getting dark out. The air around them grew still, while Captain Hank retrieved their fish dinners.

The man who was selling fish was a pirate. He recognized Captain Hank as one of Talbasta's friends. He ordered Captain Hank to give him the treasure, and held a knife to his side. Lexus and August came to his rescue each with a different plan. August cut in front of Lexus.

August took a new gold coin out of his pocket and handed it to the pirate. "Here take this, and leave him alone." The pirate unhanded Captain Hank, taking the coin in his fingers as he admired the shine.

August did not take this action lightly, as he remembered that he had given his parents each a coin on the ship before the room was engulfed in flames. Maybe it was the smoke or fire that ended their lives. However, he knew that the cause could have been the judging coins he placed in their palms. He would have to live with the emotion of that uncertainty.

The man August traded the coin with for Captain Hank's life, burst into dust, but not before acting against the group. A loud pop was sounded.

"What was that?" Lexus asked feeling something cold on his leg. He had been shot, and blood was running down his limb. Captain Hank and August grabbed Lexus and got him back to their campsite. They made him drink the treasure water.

He fought against them to save it because it had not worked on him the first time. Helena slunk next to Lexus, and he asked her, "Do you remember me from the first time you encountered the pirates? I'm the one who let you go. I'm sorry I had to pretend to be a pirate, but I wanted to go with you then. I hope you never have to pretend that you're a pirate. It causes certain death one way or another. I really like you. I know you know it, too." He squeezed her hand.

"I remember," Helena admitted.

Lexus smiled with his eyes closed. His eyes popped back open, as he grabbed both her hands. Another shot had been fired into him by a nearby pirate emerging from the dark. August threw three gold coins from his pocket at the pirate and the man turned to dust from the Judgment of the Island's treasure. Lexus laid back down, breathing a final breath, Helena was his last glimpse of life.

CHAPTER 16

Lexus, the handsome and brave boy had gone on to the next life, and Helena felt like she was missing a piece of herself. She had only known him a short time.

Avril was weary of seeing people die. She was obviously not over losing her parents, and it had not even been a full week since their disappearance.

August took a coin from his gold abundant pocket, and he placed it in the palm of Lexus's lifeless hand. He knew that the dust in the coins, when liquified, was what healed him. It was what the treasure elixir Captain Hank gave him was made from.

The coin in Lexus's lifeless hand began to glow like the starlight wishing stone. Lexus's wounds began to heal, and the bullets popped out of his chest, and the femoral artery in his leg. His skin closed over the open wounds and new blood rushed through his veins.

Lexus did not know he had died. Helena took his hand, the one without the coin in it, and Lexus opened his eyes to see his friends surrounding him. "I think I'm feeling better."

"No Lexus, you're all better," Helena explained to him. He sat up and agreed that he did not think he would die right then after all.

"Thank God," Captain Hank murmured.

August watched the gold coin in Lexus's hand vanish into dust. He realized that not all people would turn to dust, but the coins truly would judge them. With his hands in his pockets, August kept watching for pirates. He was ready to fight.

With August now off by himself, Captain Hank finally cooking the dinner, and Avril and Lexus getting to know one another; Helena slowly walked over to August.

Helena thought that August looked very handsome in the moonlight. He was throwing rocks across a little pond, while standing on a small, arched bridge that belonged to the house across the water. It was part of the drive to the house he had stumbled upon earlier.

"Hey," Helena called to August, approaching him from behind.

He did not stir or turn around, but answered back to her, "Hey."

"I could have been a pirate," she warned him with a smile, taken aback by his lackluster response. He did not look at her but he did smile, and he reached back to take her hand. She was surprised by this and found that he had placed a pebble in the palm of her hand. "I shouldn't have let the heart treasure determine my feelings for me," she admitted. He finally looked at her. Her face was bright despite the topic.

It began to rain. The cold droplets falling on Helena's cheek sent a shiver through her body.

"So how do you feel?" August asked her simply.

Helena put her head down, and shyly began to talk about him instead of answering, "You're kindhearted, understanding, strong, intense, and I have this compelling pressure on me to tell you that I love you back…"

"But?" He questioned her, as he fidgeted.

August looked, to her, as if he was anticipating a harsh response and was bracing himself. Yet Helena shrugged, and put her hands into the pockets of the forest-green jacket she had taken from him from what seemed like so long ago.

"I'm just nervous. I'm afraid – like actually really scared that one of us won't make it if we keep this treasure or stay on this island. Being with Lexus for days…" She noticed August's expression fall, as if he was trying to mask a sense of disappointment. She kept on with what she was saying, "…was like listening to a history professor for eternity, but it really opened my eyes. We are in a real danger here, and it won't ever end for us if we stay. I've heard so many stories of Graces and Lences that have helped protect the people of Talley Gulf Island. Every single one of them has a tragic end. All of them - August, and I don't want that to be us."

August let her words sink into his mind. The alternative came to him. "Helena, why does it have to be you and me? Why can't it be some other Grace and Lence – it's only our middle names - not even our first names?"

Helena saw his eyes turn red for a moment. It was a sight that she was hoping would not happen. She tilted her head and looked toward the ground, knowing it was their fate. "I don't know – can it be another or does it have to be you and me?" She asked him, hoping that the outcome would change somehow by asking him again. She wanted to lecture him, she wanted to tell him not to lie to her again, and she wanted to fight. However, Helena Grace Hank knew that they were the protectors, just as Augustine Lence Bridges knew it, too.

"Well, I guess we'll need to ask Lexus," August answered with a wide, knowing smile. Helena chuckled.

Right then it started pouring rain, in contrast to the light drizzle earlier. The booming thunder could be heard in the distance. She pulled over the jacket hood onto her head as the raindrops fell around them.

"Okay then, let's go find out." Helena started to walk away, but August pulled her back.

"One more thing," he said taking her hand and spinning her around in a short dance. Helena stepped on his foot, and though he felt the pain, he took the pain without a flinch.

Helena hid her amusement well enough, until August looked at her face. She noticed a change in the turquoise eyes she knew from the ship. There was a stateliness in his manner now that had not been there before. While she was gone, he had changed. It was as if he had stepped into his role as one of the protectors, whereas, she had not yet taken on that responsibility for herself. It was strange, the fact that now he seemed almost kingly.

The treasures they used had aged them, and their bodies were older than the years they had lived. Helena could tell August had been exposed to more of the treasures. Every treasure seemed to add a year of experience. The more they encountered, the less of a mystery it was as to why the other protectors seemed to die so young.

Helena wanted to tell August her discovery regarding seeing the red eyes, but she stopped herself. The change in August opened the door for a sense of self doubt in Helena. She was usually confident, but as August stepped into new characteristics, Helena felt a shift in her own countenance. She felt timid. The topics she wanted to divulge were sinking down into the back of her mind as irrelevant. Maybe August was the Lence, but she was not the Grace.

As August, toyed with her fingers, he felt as if Helena was finally seeing him for who he was, someone smart and willing to fight. He had always been this way, but Helena had seen him in a more sensitive and impulsive light. He wanted her to see that he was mature, and could handle their situation, while also making her feel safe and loved. If he was going to say the word, he was going to accept the responsibility just as he had accepted the responsibility of her death before he knew she was alive.

Helena did not know that August had been planning to kiss her. She was looking down, still battling with her thoughts. August interrupted the storm in her mind, as he brought her back to the reality of the rainstorm around them. He still held one of her hands in his, as he placed the other loosely on her back. He stopped guiding her as a flash of lightning gave August a better look at her saddened expression.

"What is it?" He calmly begged to know. She shook her head with the falsehood that there was nothing, and he saw her eyes turn red. He frowned in thoughtfulness, as he leaned his chin on her head, feeling as though he had intruded on her inner world. "Helena, you can tell me anything."

She danced with him in silence for a minute, as he let her think. August had learned that he was too impatient sometimes, when she just needed a moment to sort out her inner dialogue. Helena soon said, "I think I know what the red eyes mean." August slowly pulled back and wanted to hear what she had to say without disengaging from the moment they were sharing. "I think – it means the person is lying. I tested it out in the mirror, and it happened each time I spoke a lie."

"So, the healing water, is a truth serum?" August questioned, and pulled her back in. He lightly held both her arms. "Well done." He complimented her with a bright smile, only having been affected by the lifting of her spirits. He twirled her once again, melting away her conversational reservations. From her twirl, she landed against him. He admired her face, as the moonlight began to show brightly in the night sky after the rain. He kissed her.

Helena quietly whispered, "What was that?" Admiration rested in her expression, as she was pleasantly surprised despite her question.

To which he answered, "A kiss." As his words were clear, he leaned his forehead down to meet hers. "I won't ever lie to you – never again. Not even a little." He voiced with honor.

Her sweet happiness melted into a gracious acceptance of his vow. "I will do my best to find the words to express myself, too. I never want you to see my eyes red," was Helena's answer. "Even if I know it's not what you want to hear, I will be honest with you to the best of my ability." He held her. It was more about partnership than romance for her. This was the first moment she felt as if they were equals.

Soon enough, they left their misty moment in the rain to seek counsel from Lexus. They wanted to know if they truly were the only hope for the island. Could the prophetic nature of their supposed titles be given to another pair?

They joined the group sitting around the treasure map. August and Helena raised their concerns to Lexus, who gladly enacted his passion for lecturing. Captain Hank and Avril listened, as well. Lexus explained that only the two who were right for the job would be drawn in toward the treasures. The likelihood that it was some other two would be slim to none. Moreover, they would have to arrive, find partnership with one another, and be ready to protect the treasure – in four days.

"Four days?" They questioned simultaneously, with Avril and Captain Hank looking on as if it was a tennis match. Helena put her head in her hands, which August observed out of the corner of his eyes. He put a hand on Helena's back, glaring harshly at Lexus as if their fate was his fault.

August stood up, tilted his head slightly, and began to walk off. Lexus understood that he was to follow August. August let out a deep, cleansing sigh. Part of him wanted to fight Lexus, as he assumed that Helena had feelings for this person, too. August reminded himself that Lexus was still an ally.

Lexus perceived August as someone stronger and older than he was, even if August was younger than him. The treasures had aged August. Lexus had read about this phenomenon, but was not expecting it to be true. August fit the type of what the previous Lence position had portrayed him to be like, though seeing it in person was an extraordinary experience for one who understood the lore of the protectors. It was intimidating to see that the next Lence of the Island, August, wanted to fight him. Lexus was strong, too, from his faux piracy, but he was more of a scholar than a soldier. The gesture to walk with him was not in friendship, it was a challenge. "What is it?" Lexus asked August, when they were out of earshot of the others.

"**D**o me a favor, and for a moment just stop acting like you know everything," August commanded, with the mission of remaining calm.

"You asked me," Lexus defended himself with more attitude, causing August to lose his ability to hold back his rage. He took out his anger and allowed his willingness to fight Lexus to take over. He shoved him against a tree with his hand on his throat, before letting go. Lexus was tugging at his throat in pain from the strain of August's action. With vigor, he continued, "Believe me, I am sorry I can't switch *you* out with someone else. Seriously, are you that selfish that you wouldn't take this position to prevent someone else from having to bear your misfortune. I would do it myself – if I bore the right name," Lexus seethed.

"**I** would! I will..." August pointed at him, holding back his temper with fury in his eyes. "I'm not asking for me. I'm asking for Helena."

Lexus looked back toward the direction of the camp. "But you can't change it – not for you – not for her. I'm sorry, but you just can't." Lexus eyes flashed a slight reddish pink color instead of just red.

In an instant August knew, based on Helena's understanding that Lexus's words were just his opinion and not fact. Lexus could be wrong, but did not know for sure. In a calmer manner, August asked him, "You said a slim chance, but is there a possibility?" He asked standing close to Lexus's face, and talking very quietly, remembering that Helena could probably still hear them. He hoped he could still save Helena from her fate.

August's range of intensity from moment to moment left Lexus unnerved.

"It would be a miracle, Lence. Reasons it won't happen: the order you found the treasure in, you finding the map that only the kings had access to, and – and because you're wearing the ring!" Exclaimed Lexus, noticing the ring on August's hand for the first time. He grabbed August's hand and held it up in his face.

"Don't touch me." August yanked his hand back, shoving Lexus back.

Lexus rubbed his face in exasperation, as August wrung his own hands.

"All this aggression while wearing the reality ring," Lexus judged him, and kicked out August's ankle from under him. August fell to the ground in the mud.

"Well at least I'm not a liar," August stated as he tried to get back on his feet.

"I'm not a liar," Lexus exclaimed.

"Oh please! You pretended to be a pirate, of course you're a liar." August instigated, finally feeling like fighting him was the right move.

"That was to protect Helena – and you. Maybe I shouldn't have, but the judging coins seemed to have justified my actions, so why am I meant to care of your opinion?" Lexus got a few punches in as they fought. "Ammon kidnapped Helena – I saved her life – again!" Lexus's pride and anger was evident, as August knocked him down, and had him by the throat again.

"You helped the ones who killed Talbasta. In 'my opinion' you deserve to die! I don't care about what the coins say, or how many people you think you saved. How many people did you get killed while undercover?" August accused Lexus.

"It wasn't about them – it was about you two." Lexus fought back. "And what about you and your kill streak?"

"My what?" August's fury ignited further, but he was calmer still. The angrier he got; the stronger he was.

"You killed people on that ship. You're just as guilty as I am – maybe even more. I didn't fight in the 'Pirates Versus Passengers War' – you did. The only reason you haven't burst into dust, holding those coins, is because you're a Lence. God will be your judge, but you left your own parents to die on that cruise liner. I was the one who rescued them." Lexus spewed.

August's eyes widened, he let go, and stepped back. There was not a hint of red in Lexus' irises as he spoke against August. August did not trust Lexus, but he did trust Helena's discovery enough to allow Lexus to get his bearings before continuing their verbal altercation.

"Tell me what you know." August twitched. Before he could get an answer, Avril found them.

Lexus walked in the opposite direction back to the campsite ready to grab his things and say goodbye to Helena. August went after him. Lexus reached Helena and explained that he needed to stay away from August despite his call to protect them. They were not a good match as perhaps other Pages would be to their cause. Helena tried to stop him, and asked him to stay repeatedly.

When August caught up, he said, "Lexus, I'm sorry, I was wrong."

Lexus nodded in acceptance of his apology, and said, "All the same, I have some people I need to see."

"Will you please tell me what happened to them?" August begged Lexus.

Lexus did not answer, instead, he looked at Helena. "You two are together now, so you'll be safe." Lexus stated, giving Helena a gentle kiss on the cheek before leaving.

August was remorseful of his actions, even though having Lexus out of the picture was what he wanted.

Chapter 17

August had an expression of guilt on his face that did not wear off easily. He smirked at Helena trying to guard himself from her opinion. He was hoping she would not ask him anything about it, but her face begged the questions as she stared at him starkly.

"I was wrong – I falsely accused Lexus. He apparently saved my parents. At least he said he did, and he wasn't lying." August was still angry, despite being apologetic for his own actions.

He closed his eyes for a moment, remembering Helena give Lexus a kiss on the cheek earlier in the night. Then when Lexus returned the sentiment moments earlier, it made August's blood boil. It felt cruel, even if it was not a real kiss like his had been with Helena. August had to stop himself from thinking about it because he already made his promise to Helena that he would never lie to her. He sighed, "To be honest, I don't want you to see me as the bad guy, but we got in a fight. I started it." He put his head down, trying to breathe distinctively, as he confessed.

"You what?" She asked.

"He fought back ..." August clarified, "I still shouldn't have done it. I know I'm stronger."

Helena put her head down, "And that's why he left? That's why you apologized. You couldn't just be calm?"

August wanted to call her out on her hypocritical statement, she made the dumbest decisions when she was angry that somehow brought her luck instead of tragedy. His blood pressure raised, but instead he took a deep breath, understanding her stance. His actions had brought them to this point, and he said, "Fair enough."

When he stood, Helena patted him on the shoulder. They knew he was going to go retrieve Lexus despite his better judgment. It would be his fault if a pirate attacked Lexus.

He did not want that on his conscious nor did he want to miss out on the knowledge of what truly happened to his parents. He did not want to go alone; Helena went with him.

Helena was acting unnecessarily sweet to August after his actions, but August appreciated it nonetheless. Typically, she was more of a mystery, but now she was more of a partner. Her choice to be kind was despite the fact she refused to forgive August for brawling with Lexus.

They saw Lexus and called out to him. He did not turn around, and so they quickened their pace to catch up with him. As they approached him, he turned around. In this light, he appeared almost as strong as August.

"Right – hi, you two," the blonde boy said cautiously. August paused, putting his arm up gently in front of Helena, to signal for her not to get closer.

"I'm sorry, I forgot your name," August said to him, "What was it again?" Helena looked at August in confusion for a moment, but did not say anything as she glanced down to see that this boy had no bruises and cuts from his altercation with August.

"Lexus," the boy answered slowly. Both August and Helena saw differently in his eyes, as they turned red, giving away his lie. This was Mark, Lexus's identical twin brother. Helena whispered in August's ear. August nodded in alignment, looking down at her with a slight grin, making her feel more secure. Safety, was something she felt with August more than she did when she was with Lexus. Even though Lexus always had a plan, it always led them to more danger.

August slyly asked the boy in front of them, "Why did you leave?"

"Well, you know me – the reason is obvious." Mark answered.

Helena rolled her eyes and blatantly asked him, "Where is Lexus?" August looked down at her, taken back by her ignoring his lead, but reeled in his facial expressions to present them as a united front. "Don't even pretend you're not – we can tell the difference." She slickly concluded, squinting in the sunlight on the hill. "Tell us where your brother is."

Helena pulled out her knife, as quickly as Mark had reached for his pocket.

"Tell us what you know," she instructed Mark, insisting that he tell them about where Lexus was because there was no way it was a coincidence that he was there. She also insisted on knowing the plans of the pirates.

"The pirates aren't planning anything after you killed most of the leaders on that boat of yours," Mark snapped, looking at August, not Helena.

August looked through his belongings and the treasures he carried, as Helena guarded him, and continued to question him about what he was doing and why he was out there. "Going to the boat," Mark answered, glaring at Helena as she glared back.

"Why?" Helena asked him, closely, so that he could feel the blade.

"I'm going to see if any of them survived." He answered.

August stopped searching for a moment, and stood in front of Mark with no use of weapons but his now imposing stature. "Explain further."

"I'm going there to kill them," Mark responded simply. August glanced at Helena, taking his eyes off Mark for a moment. Neither one of them had seen if he was lying or not.

Mark decided to risk trying to run away with his bag. August handed Helena the gun he had found in Mark's possessions. Helena went after him. Mark expected the gun to still be with him in his bag, but when he reached for it, he could not feel it. He dropped the bag to try to trip Helena Hank. Managing to hop over the bag, she pulled the trigger of the gun shooting Mark in the leg as his brother Lexus had been shot in the leg. August was behind her.

"Where did you think you were going?" August questioned him. "We weren't done talking. Why would you kill the survivors of your own people?"

"Why did you shoot at me? I have to go!" Mark exclaimed, worried as ever as he grabbed his leg in throbbing anguish.

"You were running away," August said simply. "You are a pirate – are you not?"

"They are going to kill my brother," was the answer they received from Mark. August and Helena peered over at each other. "They found out about him saving you." Mark pointed at Helena. "They want him dead." August's guilt regarding Lexus crept back into his heart and onto his face. "Plus, he stole your treasure map." They hid their shock at this revelation and kept the interrogation going.

"Why are you so concerned about saving him? Aren't pirates usually self-interested?" August challenged him.

"My brother and I are identical twins, and they don't know there are two of us. A threat on his life is a threat on mine. We are one in the same to the pirates. They will go after him and I know this well enough because they already have. One of the old waiters on the ship dislocated my shoulder earlier today," he answered them.

Helena and August knew he was not lying, but Helena pushed him further knowing that he did not know they could tell. "Great story, Mark, the only problem is your intentions are not good." August tied Mark up, as Helena dressed his wound.

"Don't worry, 'bro', we'll protect *Mark* for you." August patted Mark's dislocated shoulder with a smirk, as a call back to Mark pretending to be his brother Lexus. "Come on, Helena, we need to go find the other brother."

"You two can't stop them. That's not your fate," the defeated boy stated to them as a last warning. Helena brilliantly smiled as they were already walking away, but she heard him nonetheless, in his albeit quiet confession.

"So, you can tell when people are lying *and* if their intentions are good now, can you?" August mocked her as he jokingly laughed.

"You would still be back on the boat dying of an injury if I didn't have that power," she humorously bantered with him back.

"Right. Right." For a brief time, his sternness lessened as his brightness shone due to Helena being in his presence with a smile. His mouth tightened, as he looked toward the distance, and he said, "Let's find Lexus before you find another reason to like me." His mouth slipped into a grin, as he continued to sarcastically tease her.

H elena was struck by how handsome he had become. "Okay," she agreed simply.

B oth could feel the other one had something they were holding back.

He looked down at his hand again, and the ring sparkled in the sunlight. He was still unsure of what it did, but just as he had been acting differently, he felt that Helena had been looking at him differently, too, since he put it on. He knew something that he had not mentioned to Helena. They were both wearing treasure rings. He had noticed it on her hand when she pulled out her knife earlier. She was wearing the expanding glass circle. One of Helena's gifts, from the treasure, truly was to be able to tell if someone's intentions were good or bad.

August and Helena's thoughts were beginning to align more closely as they remained together. August had a suspicion that many of the couples of 'Lence and Grace's positions had felt as they did now. He and Helena were not yet ready for whatever it was that they were about to face. They still had no idea why Lexus took the map, aside from that he could be taking it to the other Pages. He did seem to be bothered by August, Helena, Avril, and Captain Hank having possession of the royal map in the first place. There was also still the mystery of the countdown and what was going to happen in four days.

CHAPTER 18

"Wait!" A shout was heard behind them. Mark was attempting to stand to his feet. He wabbled as he said, "Please heal me, before you leave me here? I will renounce piracy if you save me." August Bridges turned sharply to see Mark on the hill. Mark's eyes were not red, so August gestured for Helena to stay. Mark continued to shout from the hill, "If I'm not telling the truth – you can place a judging coin in my hand. I will accept the consequences." August approached him.

Helena, was waiting for August to show him mercy, but she was annoyed about how much longer it was taking. She continued their search for Lexus. It was daylight, and there was less of a threat of being attacked by pirates right now. She called out repeatedly for Lexus.

Mark observed the annoyed and guilt-ridden acceptance on August's face. He wanted to know why the woman who should be famously loyal only to the Lence was calling out for someone else. It was obvious that whatever transpired was August's fault. "What did you do?" He curiously questioned with a familiar, coy smile.

"Nothing that concerns you," August gave Mark a warning glare as he cut him loose. "We can't heal you, but we can take you back to our camp to rest. At least give you a chance against the other pirates. It's better than leaving you here to die." Mark nodded eagerly in agreement, understanding that this was August's version of a threat. If he kept taunting the Lence, he would be left to his fate.

Helena unwaveringly suggested to August, "You take Mark back – I'll try to find Lexus. I think I know where he was going." August was trying not to let it get to him, that Helena was so concerned about Lexus, but it still bothered him. Helena took off through the brush, leaving August with Mark. August allowed Mark to hobble along with him back to their camp on Talbasta's property.

Once again, Captain Hank was angry with August for letting Helena go trouncing off by herself in 'pirate infested territory.' With a deep breath and a judgmental shake of his head, Captain Hank went to find his daughter. He recalled the recurring dream he used to have when on the ship. He recalled that in the dream August would stand with a sword in the sand on the island, in between Helena and the pirates. He had yet to see this come to fruition.

No one explained to Avril that the young man, who was with them now, was Mark and not Lexus. August quickly rattled off a request for Avril to help him with his injuries, before attempting to catch up with Captain Hank who had already left. Aside from the obvious gunshot wound, Avril assumed the injuries in question, were ones that August and Lexus's fight had caused. Avril had no reason to believe the person before her was not Lexus. "You got shot again?" Avril asked him with stifled amusement, when the others were gone.

Mark was surprised by her candor, and matched her humorous tone, "Aye – well when it happens enough you get used to it." He shrugged his shoulders, playfully. "Plus, it is kind of ruggedly charming, don't you think?" He smirked.

"How's that?" Avril laughed at his self-assured comment, though she could not deny he was charming, mostly because he was so handsome. Mark was an inch taller than Lexus, and did not have any tattoos like his brother did. He parted his hair in a different way, but aside from those aspects they looked identical.

"All the girls like to hear my stories," he stated, sitting up as tall as he could, while posing. He did this in an obvious way to make her laugh.

"Yes, they like stories... of you getting shot." Avril pointed out with a raised eyebrow. His eyes twinkled at her clever insult.

"It makes me sound tough," smiled the boy, correcting her assessment. "You think I'm charming, don't you? Or do you think I'm unlucky?" There was a slight genuine curiosity in his question, although he was still flirting.

"Well, your cadence is charming. However, you are certainly unlucky," Avril said, handing him a bottle of water. His hands seem rougher now than when she shook his hand when they met. Avril noticed he was wearing less symbolic jewelry, as well.

"Thank you," Mark said thoughtfully, breaking her concentration, "even if I am un-lucky – you at least think I'm handsome, right?"

"It wouldn't matter if you were, if your gift is charm," she answered.

Mark's smile spread from ear to ear as he leaned back in the sand, resting his leg as he enjoyed the good company. The silence of everything, but treasure and waves sounded so peaceful to him. He rested his eyes, and mentally retired as a pirate – at least for the time being.

Avril sat by him in the sand as he slept, after triaging his leg. She was no Helena Hank, but she did her best to help him. He was motionless and she was bored. Her thoughts were racing. Avril was worried that at any moment the young man would stop breathing, due to the distress she had witnessed lately. The stress wore her out, and she was fighting to stay awake as she sat in the sun, keeping watch over him.

Helena, August, and Captain Hank were now together, searching for Lexus but having no luck in the least. They kept tripping on sticks and stones. Their faces cleared the fresh spider webs spread between the branches in the trees. Everyone grew tired and hungry.

Helena longed for sleep; August longed for more food. They were jealous of Avril and Mark who were most likely back at the campsite resting and eating.

"Hopefully Avril and Mark are taking shifts in protecting the treasures that are back at the camp," Captain Hank finally spoke, as he was getting annoyed with their whining.

Meanwhile, Avril was still awake, fighting her battle against sleep. Mark finally woke up to see her unrested for his convenience. He was apologetic to her, and was moved by her kindness of letting him rest. "You rest now. I'll watch over things. Will you hand me one of the guns? Just in case the pirates come..." Mark suggested to Avril.

She presented him with a weapon, and quickly faded off to sleep as Mark enjoyed the majestic sunset. For a moment he glanced over at Avril, thinking she was beautiful. He grinned at the thought of protecting her and was amused that she trusted him to watch over her. He assumed she knew what he was.

When Avril woke up from her nap, Mark asked her about various topics from what was her favorite color to her shoe size, to if she liked pirates who gave up their piracy. She did not realize that was a real question to see if she liked him. They laughed and talked together as if they had known each other all their lives. He listened attentively to every answer she gave.

"I thought you were different then you are – when we first met," she told him and he was puzzled.

"Do you – no longer think I'm charming?" He asked.

"I mean when you were shot the first time – I thought you liked Helena," Avril admitted. Mark was confused. "And you just seemed a little more distant with me – a little uncomfortable. Now you don't seem to be that way – if that makes sense," she shared. "I just thought I'd mention it."

"Thank you," he said, but added, "Why would you think I would be interested in Helena? She's a Grace - destined to be with a Lence. I would really have to hate myself to willingly fall for a Grace." He chuckled, starting to realize what was happening, as he mentally judged his brother. This must have been why August seemed so upset by Lexus. Mark smiled as he put the puzzle pieces together.

"I don't know," Avril responded to his comment, "I just thought you liked her."

"Do you know my name?" Mark asked her after pausing for a moment.

"Lexus," she said.

Mark added onto her answer, "... is my brother. I'm sorry, but you have mistaken me for my twin brother, Lexus. My name is Mark." Avril was surprised by the situation and felt very nervous. She had been left by herself with a stranger she only knew the face of, and her family, friends, and parental figure were so far away. Her jitters increased. The silent response made Mark uneasy. There was no sign of Helena or the search party.

"Um, I don't mean to pry or make you feel uncomfortable or anything, but you never told me your name – either. I am Lexus's brother so it's not like we're total strangers; I am a friend. You can trust me. Your brother trusted me, or he would not have left me here with you. What is your name?" Mark asked carefully. Not knowing if she had heard of what he truly was.

"My brother left you here with me, not me here with you. My brother trusts me regardless of if he trusts you. I'm Avril," she corrected him as she answered him.

"Right, of course." He shook her hand. Their conversation slowly began again as they waited for the others to return.

As these occurrences took place with the different groups on the shore of the island and in the forest, there was a loner who had fallen in a shallow hole – Lexus.

CHAPTER 19

When Lexus woke up, he quietly cursed himself about how ridiculous it was that he had fallen. It was nearly nightfall. "Help!" He yelled out, "If anyone is out there – I've fallen into a hole." His admission of this statement made him laugh, and he began to try to climb out, but could not. He sighed deeply, knowing he must have hit his head as it was throbbing. They were closer to the door to where his society was located.

However, there lived a farmer nearby who grew fruit trees, and he happened to hear Lexus's plea for rescue. The man did not speak the same language as Lexus. 'Motonoikchey,' was spoken by island natives. The man who saved Lexus spoke the oldest dialect known, it was different than what Lexus knew, but it was close enough to be understood. In the known world, it was closest to Greek.

Lexus was pulled out of the hole. The man who saved him, introduced himself, "My name is Teddy. This is my farm." He firmly grasped the shoulders of the young man, dusting him off quickly. Teddy saw the symbols of the Page society around the young man's neck, wrist, and fingers. He handed Lexus a piece of fruit from his property.

Lexus's own luck in being saved, worried him, as he did not trust coincidences due to his knowledge of prophecies on the island. He was concerned that he stepped into the beginning of a prediction he had been avoiding for quite some time.

Teddy checked to see if Lexus had any broken bones, sprains, or a concussion. He did not know if Lexus was a pirate or on the side of the protectors, as the symbols Lexus wore represented a group of Oracles from the Corazana line that had been corrupted by pirates. They had been slain at the same time as the royals were dethroned. The Pages had been a secret society long before the Oracles, but it was in fact – a secret. They shared the same symbols and knew the same prophecies, but their translations were vastly different. There was one prophecy that Lexus was more familiar with than any other Page, and this was the one that constantly worried him.

Teddy decided to take a bold risk, to test if Lexus was a pirate or not. "I'll tell you a secret. I was Talbasta's uncle. His mother was my sister. She was a Grace. Because of my involvement in her cause - I can also see the treasures." Lexus was surprised by the fruit farmer's transparency. It was rare for Lexus to find anyone who had knowledge about the island.

Teddy pointed at the symbol on Lexus's necklace. "The information passed down to you, you learned from stolen information and translations made by pirates. The royals knew the truth of the words you study."

Lexus took Teddy's words as an insult, but he answered calmly, "I didn't have the luxury of having my parents to teach me anything." Lexus rolled up his sleeve, revealing a more detailed story in the form of a tattoo.

"The Fate of The Flower ..." Teddy furrowed his brow in awe, as he took a closer look at the young man's arm. He looked up at Lexus, suddenly in shock that the two of them were speaking. This was the title of the most famous prophecy known on the island, but the title was not written on Lexus's arm. The prophecy was tattooed in symbols on his skin. It appeared that he received them when he was very young, as the markings were stretched.

The design was of a cloud covered sun with footprints going off toward a crescent moon. There were flowers lining the edge. There was a crown set upon the Talley Gulf Treasure, and a sword set in the sand. Teddy knew the prophecy; it was the first dream recorded from the first pirate.

Dreams were not possible on or around Talley Gulf Island because of the properties belonging to the island and the treasures. The last person to have a dream before Captain Hank or August Bridges, was the first pirate – Prince Pale. Lexus and Mark were descended from the royal family on the island – specifically – Prince Pale's line. Their fate would mirror the first pirate's dream.

The Pages, islanders, and royals all considered Prince Pale's dreams to be prophecies, as they usually came to pass, despite his stained reputation. Pale had written them all down in a text. The full text of Pale's dreams included the royal map in it, but it was torn out and fought over for generations. The castle the royals lived, was burned down by pirates who sought out the map. The pirates believed what the Oracles suggested, which was they should inherit the island and the treasures.

History suggested that Pale's contact with the treasures distorted his personality. His emotions were never restored until the end of his life when he found and wore the reality ring. He was placed in exile, on the island, until the King killed him.

Teddy recited the translation of the prophecy that no one else knew, *"One twin is taken by Pale's followers, as the April flower is made a princess of Pale. The Flower wields her will unknowingly until The Lence sets his sword in the sand for an era. The Grace returns for her crown before the flower and the twin are freed from their fates..."* Teddy looked up at Lexus, hoping the answer was not as clear as it seemed, and he asked, "Why do you have this tattoo?"

Lexus looked at the man with heavy eyes. "This was done to me when my brother and I were born. My brother had the symbol of a tree on his arm. The origins of the treasure tree that spread its gifts throughout the island. Since he had the source of the treasure as a birthmark on his skin, it was assumed that I would be the pirate. They were wrong. He became a pirate and I did not."

Teddy felt pity for Lexus. It was a heavy prophecy. Lexus and his brother Mark were destined to be two halves of the same coin – the two halves of the moon. The common understanding was that one of them would be a protector and the other would be a pirate. However, those who studied the dreams carefully knew that one of them would eventually betray the crown and steal a woman from the Lence in power.

Lexus continued a little bewildered, "My brother was the one who told the pirate captain about Captain Hank's deal with Talbasta. He led them to the ship. I assumed that was when the prophecy was going to take place. He was supposed to take the April flower, the Lence's sister, and marry her. She was supposed to be taken and turned to piracy. He never took her; the other pirates did and then she was freed. Avril never became a pirate..."

Avril's fate was that she was meant to be stolen by his pirate brother. However, it never happened, and Lexus darkly realized it was he who was the one stealing from the Lence. He wanted Helena. If Helena married him – she would be married to someone royal, but also someone from the bloodline of pirates. He wanted to take Helena from the Lence. He was almost relieved that the path that would lead to death was not meant for his brother Mark, but for himself.

He did not share his realization out loud, and both men were silent for a moment until Teddy spoke, "I see it was your destiny to come here. This place – is the house of Pale's exile. You could apprentice here, avoid you and your brother's fates for as long as you can." Teddy said. "That's my house, it once belonged to Pale." He pointed to a small villa in the distance.

"You want me to be an apprentice - on your farm?" Lexus curiously questioned.

Teddy shortly pointed out, "There is more to this place than a farm. The treasures grow here." Teddy answered.

Lexus put his head down. "There is only four days left now before Augustine Bridges becomes an official Lence… I can try to hide here, but the prophecy will come to pass."

Teddy shook his head. "I may not like your society of Oracles, but you have a right to be here, to rest, before the flower is taken by the half of the moon. Though the new Lence and his sister are descendants of the island, unlike many of the protectors and their families that come from around the world, I know you and your brother are the last ones to remain from the royal bloodline. I may not believe that someone born from piracy should inherit the island or the treasures, but I do believe in the significance of the royal family to the island. You and the Lence have much in common. You are both tied closely to the source of the treasures."

"It may be a long time before the island will be safe again," Lexus answered him, referring to the second part of the prophecy, where the sword is used on Talley Gulf Island for what was noted as 'a young lifetime,' and no one was sure how many years that meant. It meant that the pirates would be prominent for a long while if the 'flower' was stolen away. "How do I know I can trust you? The society will wonder what happen to me – if I stay here."

"For this reason." Teddy reached to his eyes, and took out his contact lenses, revealing an alarming yet fantastic sight. Teddy's eye color was a continually shifting color between red and purple. "I have sipped the healing water when nothing was wrong with me, and this was the result. All I have to do is think of telling a lie and my eyes shift to red."

Lexus was shocked and thought of Helena, as he knew her secret ability from the treasure. He had known before August knew, and he sighed, "Why can I see that?"

Teddy was very good at gathering secret intel quickly. He divulged, "The Grace's eyes turn red when she lies. Anyone can see it. Whereas, if you were to lie – only she would see your eyes turn red. Sometimes it shows up on camera's too, but a lot of people think it's a trick of the light. Better that they believe it, too. I moved out here to avoid eye contact with too many people."

Lexus could understand why the man would not want people to stare at him constantly, as he was doing now. He looked away not wanting to gawk, as he knew how it felt due to his unique tattoo. Lexus asked how Teddy knew about Helena's gift.

"The hole you fell into was from a space I dug up. It was where I found a treasure – buried here on this farm. See, it's a good place to apprentice." Teddy smiled. Lexus was obsessive when it came to learning information. He was almost as passionate about learning as he was about lecturing. He leaped at the chance to see this exclusive treasure Teddy told him about.

He could not hide his disappointment upon seeing the treasure – it was a stick. It was brown, pointed, and straight as any other. He sighed.

Teddy did not appreciate his reaction or his attitude. He asked Lexus to give him one reason that the branch was not good enough.

Lexus sharply responded, "It is not like any of the other pieces. It is supposed to be Talley Gulf *Treasure*, not lawn waste. The real ones – they shine, and this stick has no glow. Sorry, but I do not believe you even if you believe it in your eyes."

"This branch – very similarly to this farm – is more than meets the eye," Teddy corrected him. "You have a lot to learn."

Chapter 20

Captain Hank, August, and Helena were making their way back to Talbasta's home, unable to find Lexus. Helena watched the ground as she took every step. Her hair kept getting into her eyes because her hairpin was still left in Talbasta's house somewhere. She was having quite a bit of trouble managing it. August noticed.

As they were walking, August pulled some tall grasses, and weaved together a steady headband. It had tiny leaves on it, and on their next water break, August approached Helena, placing it on her head. It worked, and kept her hair out of her eyes. August said to her, "You don't have to thank me or anything I just noticed you were having a bit of trouble with your hair." He grinned at her, but she was looking down with a slight blush in her cheeks.

As he began to walk away from her, she said, "Thanks anyways, August Lence."

He breathed in deeply, with a relieved expression "You're welcome, Helena Grace."

Captain Hank rolled his eyes.

August knew how he looked to everyone else who saw him with Helena, but he knew he would never change. He cared for her from the beginning. He was willing to look a little foolish to do what he wanted.

Helena joined her father, as they stopped to rest, holding both sadness and joy in her expression at once. Hank looked at his daughter's face. "Why are you not hanging out with your little friend?" He pointed towards August.

She looked at him, judging his wording. "I missed my dad is all," she mumbled. Captain Hank was silent, he smiled as Helena leaned her head on him, and he put his arm around her shoulders. She was there for comfort, not a lecture or advice. He provided her with what she needed, her father.

When she finally spoke, she said, "I think I liked him when we were first on the boat, but he's different now. He's changed. I'm not sure how I feel about it. He's kind like he was before, but now he seems to have this heaviness - darkness?"

"No," Captain Hank disagreed gently. "When we first saw him on the boat – he was a survivor of a traumatic event – still in shock. Now he's a survivor of more trauma and the repercussions of the treasures. This is who he was before we knew him, but with a little more age. You both have learned a lot since you met."

"Maybe it's just my imagination that he changed," Helena wrote it off, but heard Captain Hank chuckle.

"Nah, I don't think it's your overactive imagination. I just think you should have a little more grace with him, Helena. Don't let miscommunication get in the way of your friendship." She looked at her father with a knowing expression. "It's *friendship*, you hear me?" He pointed at her. "Now go talk to him." He rolled his eyes with a loving sigh.

"I don't want to talk to him right now, talk to him for me. Will you?" Helena suggested.

Captain Hank's eyes widened. "What? I don't think I could do that."

"Please? Please, Dad?" She pleaded.

"But I don't know anything going on with you two, what would I say?" His voice went slightly higher than his naturally lower register. "I don't know why you two aren't talking. Were you not just talking over there? I'm too lost."

"Thanks, Dad." Helena did not accept a refusal, and she ignored her father's words, hugging him tightly and walking away quickly. He was left sitting alone. Captain Hank laughed to himself about his daughter, but then sat in silence for a moment a little stunned. He was not understanding how he got roped into the teen drama of potential magic-island-protectors. He clenched his jaw, swallowed hard, and took a deep sigh. Mustering up his strength to deal with teenagers, he stood up.

"August come here, please," Captain Hank commanded.

August was still greatly intimidated by Captain Hank, even after the treasures had made him more formidable. Captain Hank still had one of those faces. He had piercing blue eyes, deep wrinkles, and was stronger than he looked.

August walked over to Captain Hank. Captain Hank looked like he was about to say something, but simply gestured for August to follow him. He stopped himself from speaking to August and looked off instead. "Look," he finally spoke after a deep breath, "I'm gonna cut to the chase." August glanced at him out of the corner of his eye. Based on this interaction so far, he did not believe him. "You seem like – a nice kid. I like you – Lord knows Helena likes you..." Captain Hank struggled further with a shake of his head and stopped.

Captain Hank sighed again, realizing he had no idea what his daughter wanted him to say, so he said what he wanted to say instead.

August was stuck on the last sentence he heard about Helena liking him, and only heard Captain Hank say, "...she is a delicate, albeit fiery, person - and the best part is she is my daughter!"

Captain Hank stopped in his tracks, "Why should I let you near her again?" He had completely lost track of what he was saying, and was looking harshly at August.

"I'm sorry?" August dared to ask, as if he wanted the man to repeat himself.

Captain Hank looked away from August, happy he could reword whatever he was trying to say. The father tried again with a refreshed statement, "If you *like* my daughter - treat her well or I'll kill you." He pointed starkly at August's face.

As he turned back, he remembered the point of why he was supposed to talk to the teenager. "Oh, and one more thing – she thinks you have changed since you two have been apart. So – basically, fix it." Captain Hank commanded.

"I didn't know she felt that way," August quietly spoke, as he trailed behind Captain Hank. The man rolled his eyes and turned back around, truly not wanting to talk about this, but it sounded as if August was going to make this harder than it needed to be for him. "She doesn't share much, does she?" August asked him, which was a different response than the man was expecting.

Hank recoiled his neck a bit, "No, she is a Hank. We have been known for not talking about things. She's never been big on feelings – she wants to be a strong, tough surgeon one day. She doesn't think there's room to be emotional in surgery – it's not part of the job," Captain Hank explained thoughtfully and clearly.

This was probably the most he had ever spoken to August since they met. Captain Hank gave a compassionate smirk to the kid. He looked down on him closely, with a very serious look. "August, she is probably struggling with the image of the doctors she emulates. She may think they can handle their emotions better than she can, and that would bother her. I can guarantee you – that is probably what she is thinking."

August looked up past Captain Hank to see Helena. He could hear music in his head, and did not know if it was his imagination, the treasures, or the literal heavens opening for him. His eyes danced as his smile returned. His heart raced. He turned his face back to Captain Hank. "Thank you, Sir, for sharing that with me. I promise you; I will treat her well as you said. I will also do my best not to upset her."

Captain Hank smiled with a small chuckle at his last comment, as he patted August on the shoulder. "You two are just friends." Captain Hank lightly solidified with a threatening undertone.

However, August took off running toward Helena, only stopping to pluck a marigold from the ground to give to her. He took her into his arms. Hugging her like he had never hugged anyone before, nor would he hug anyone else like this after her. Not too strong or loose, but mending. The sentiment was returned, instead of being pushed away as August had initially anticipated.

"Marigolds are my favorite," she spoke softly as she pulled away. Helena kept herself and her emotions in check, but August could see how happy she was right beneath the surface. Helena had not noticed the wild marigolds growing, but she took it as a sign, as she always had growing up, that she was on the right path. It almost solidified her choice to want to be with August over Lexus.

Helena slid the marigold into the crown of leaves that August had fashioned for her.

Captain Hank still saw the little girl that he and his wife had separately raised, even though his daughter was almost eighteen now. Helena seemed even younger with a bright flower in her hand. Prophecy or not, Captain Hank did not want them to be married for a long time. The only thing he would allow was a partnership, and a promised unification. He did not know what the threat of four days would bring, but he would have it his way or no way at all.

Chapter 21

Walking the long-distance back was tiring, but worth it when they encountered Teddy. The man informed them that Lexus was safe back on his farm after a fall. Helena was worried, but could tell that the man was telling the truth. Teddy carried the treasure branch with him, as he had begun fashioning it into a staff for the Lence.

Helena knew she would see Lexus again, even if Lexus stayed on Teddy's land, for a little while longer, to learn. Lexus thrived on knowledge.

The group continued their journey past large rocks, snakes, and various birds. Teddy had gone with them. August could feel Helena's temperament like the change in the wind. Helena, being well rested, but thoughtful about Lexus, despite the marigold on her head, walked ahead of the others to think.

The men walked together, as Helena kept to herself, as she currently did not look approachable, but rough. This expression differed from the one she usually carried, and troubled August slightly. August was disappointed that Lexus was not with Teddy, as he still felt the guilt of his actions weighing down on him. Whereas, Helena's temperaments unnerved him less so than they used to, as now he truly could tell any shift in her feelings. He could feel the change, even while walking behind her, to the point where he could feel how out of place her thoughts were.

Maybe this was part of the four days that Lexus had forewarned? Maybe the Lence and Grace would truly have no choice but be together. He mentally admitted to himself, that it already felt like she was a part of him. He could feel her feelings, but not think her thoughts... at least... not yet.

August quickened his pace to catch up with her, giving her a look that was returned out of the corner of her eye. August's attention drifted to the ground.

Helena felt the tension of his thoughts, though she could not know what they were. The tension was pushing August closer to confrontation. They kept exchanging glances back and forth. His eagerness to gain the knowledge of her thoughts increased with her willingness to keep his at bay.

Despite their efforts, it was destiny, and their thoughts became vivid to one another. They both stopped in their tracks, turning to face one another.

Helena looked into August's eyes, while squinting hers. In her mind she thought, *"Staring at me is not going to help you read my thoughts."* This was a test to see if he could read her mind, to which August swallowed roughly.

August said aloud, "Sorry – I just…"

Helena could not tell by his answer if it was in response to her statement or not, so she tried again, *"Let me guess – you're thinking 'What's wrong with Helena now? We just had a heart to heart. I gave her a marigold…"*

"This has nothing to do with me thinking anything is wrong with you. I just feel like we – are somehow closer…" He answered once again aloud. His brow furrowed not realizing he had answered her mind.

"Don't talk," she stated, without saying a word more about what was bothering her, and instead cleverly pushed him to use his mind. *"If you can hear me now – I am showing you a secret in my mind."* She closed her eyes, picturing a memory of when she was little – the spot on her side where her mother would tickle her to make her giggle. August could see it. A sense of bewilderment shown on his face. *"Point to the place – if you can hear me,"* Helena thought. August took a deep inhale, moving his hand slowly – pointing above her right hip."

"How?" His question whispered aloud, again.

She pressed her fingers to his lips, "Try it."

This ability did not seem to be one that came from treasure, but because of who they were, and the days drawing near as they became who they were meant to be. Moreover, what would happen in the remainder of the four days?

"There is a river down the hill," Teddy interrupted them, "time for a break." They went down to the water, and Helena took her hidden weapons off, kept the ring on, and took off what she felt comfortable with to swim a little, as August did the same.

Captain Hank and Teddy had some food, while the teens swam.

As their water games brought them figuratively back to their ages for a moment, August picked her up in his arms and threw her in the water. Helena protested with splashes, as she coughed, until he had to shut his eyes. She tried to get away, to climb out, but he playfully pulled her back in. He decided to use her secret against her and tickle her until she could not breathe from laughter, but he kept her head above water when she could not hold herself up anymore. He stopped. She threw her hair straight back behind her to see, resting her hands on his shoulders to gain her composure. Her feet did not touch the sand at the bottom of the river, as his did. He held her up asking, with concern but mischief, "Are you alright?"

"I think so." She splashed him again with a flick of water, spraying him in the face. He winced with a deserving smile. Both out of breath, they looked at one another.

August started to say the words Helena knew he was thinking, "Helena…" He started.

"No," Helena moved past him. She headed toward a boulder on the edge of the water. August's head was filled with elements of the impending responsibility of the island, even in a moment when they were supposed to be having fun. Helena did not approve of his new sense of duty and responsibility. He had taken well to his fate, and she was not ready to give up her dream of becoming a doctor.

August could see it in her head, and what Helena could see in his was him keeping his family safe even if that meant wearing a crown, as the prophecy suggested.

August and Helena sat on the boulder, drying off. Unfortunately, August was determined to have the conversation about their fates. Helena was resolute not to divulge in this conversation.

The two knew how they felt about each other. However, for August it was not all about Helena, their circumstances affected his sister and now possibly his parents. He still needed to find Lexus again to reunite his family, as Lexus suggested he knew where August's and Avril's parents were. August was putting an entire island of people before the person he loved, even if he was asking her to protect it with him. That request felt insurmountable.

He spoke, despite her being able to see his thoughts, "I don't want you to be mad…" He sighed. "I have been thinking about my parents." He put his hand near hers, but she pulled hers away.

In the back of her mind Helena still thought of when August had let go of her hand, even if it was petty.

"Without us – the pirates return," he solidified frankly, but as he saw her close her eyes and lift her face to the sky; he silenced his mind to see hers. Aside from the surreal beauty around them, the treks, and the treasure that she enjoyed - Helena had a colder call. Her call was to the sterile streaks of white hallways with hollow hearts that fought death daily. She would be the one to mend them, and if she stayed, she would have to risk her future in science by using mystical objects to save others. She would have to learn a different way, and be enveloped by a culture that was not her own, nor one she wanted to be acquainted with – no one knew of this place, Talley Gulf Island.

Helena would rarely see her family. She knew her father had the intention of going back to England. Her mother and father would potentially get back together. That was the life she wished for them to have and she would be here with August.

The thought occurred to her, that maybe she could be the founder of medicine on the island – if forced to stay, and combine medicine with the mystic treasures. She could work with Lexus. On that note, August looked away from her mind.

"I didn't mean anything by that," she spoke as she felt him leave her mind. A slight expression of guilt on her face for thinking of Lexus as important to her, but it was true. She knew that she would still need a degree before even considering working with him – even if she did have to marry August to save the island from pirates. "We made a promise, August, that we would be honest," Helena retorted. "I do not want to be expected to marry you. Lexus told me the stories."

August was quiet for a moment. He thought, *"Having to marry me or be a Grace now - would automatically mean you would be trapped here, giving up your dream."*

He spoke aloud, "I have to find my family. I know I have to fix this mess of an island, and I will love you – no matter what you choose. No matter how much you love other things or other people. I will love you for you. If I can let you leave – I will. I'll fight for the both of us here, while you go." August confessed.

He took her hand gently; he could see his own actions at Talbasta's house when he had dropped it before. She winced not meaning to think of it. He was surprised, he did not realize he had done it, but he did not have full range of his emotions back then.

Helena spoke, looking him in the eye before he had a chance to say anything, "We don't have to forget who we are or what we have done, but we shouldn't dwell," she said. He exhaled deeply, as he looked at her hand in his. "I know what you mean," she responded to his apologetic face.

"Move forward," he said.

"Move forward," she agreed, fighting a tear in her eye.

Despite their differences they supported one another. They trusted each other, now more than ever as they could see inside each other's minds. Almost nothing was off limits, as they did not even know how to block the other out. They only knew how to enter and exit, nothing more. It was like a sixth sense.

That night as the group ate dinner together, August was distracted by his thoughts, as he ate. "Something bothering you, kid?" Captain Hank asked him.

"No," August answered quickly.

"Oh, okay because I was thinking about going home after this long pirate ridden adventure. I can't wait to see how happy Madison, Helena's mother, will be to see her again." Captain Hank stated with a grin. This was the first time he looked like Helena; they had the same crooked, bright smile.

"What's your wife like?" August asked him politely.

"A bunch like Helena – to be honest. Smart, adventurous, and sure of herself with a mind for science. Madison and I got married young, very young. As soon as we were legally old enough." Captain Hank answered, which got August's attention.

"Really? What was that like?" August asked him nervously.

"Well, we met one summer and thought we were in love and we wanted to get married. Well, at the time in our country it was legal to get married when you were sixteen – that's when we were married." August's eyes widen at that information. Captain Hank chuckled, and shook his head. "It wasn't right, but that's the truth. The law changed just a few years ago. I'm glad for it because I wouldn't let that happen to my daughter." He leaned in. "To be clear, my daughter will not marry young especially not for a prophecy. When she's old enough, hopefully she will choose someone decent." He eyed August.

August heard Captain Hank clearly, and agreed with him. He wanted Helena to be able to leave the island, August noticed that Captain Hank kept looking at his watch, and had been a lot lately. Helena's father caught August's glance.

Captain Hank stated, "Augustine, you should know that I have known your parents for a long time. In fact, your father and I have been best mates since you were born. He's the reason I met and married Madison. We moved here and had Helena."

Helena overheard this conversation, and with haste she joined them and asked, "I was born here, on Talley Gulf Island?"

August's eyes were also wide.

"We lived here until you were five," Captain Hank answered her. "Thadius and Belle were expecting a boy, and we thought it would be nice to raise our families together. I did not know that you two were going to be the next protectors, until we had to leave the island." He looked at August when he said it.

"Then why don't we know each other?" Helena asked. "We are only meeting now."

Captain Hank sighed before answering, "Augustine Thadius Lence Bridges, your parents were from the first family of this island. Before there was a royal family here, there were the Bridges that protected the source of the treasure. There was a Lence and a Grace and there were Pages. It was all set up for you to inherit the island and take it back from the pirates. Your parents asked me to name my daughter Grace, and though I did not know why, I made it Helena's middle name because I saw it in a dream. Everything was in line until the pirates came back, when the last of the royal line was killed. Your cousin, Talbasta took possession of the treasure to make sure it was all safely hidden with the right people. That is how I ended up with the healing water, and he explained how it worked to me. I haven't been able to see my best friend, Thadius, for almost eighteen years. I couldn't risk blowing their cover and jeopardizing your safety and my daughter's safety. Her being tied to your family was a threat to her well-being. Leaving was the only way our families could ensure the survival of the island," he admitted.

All of this was extraordinary, but it felt right and made sense now. "The thing that no one will tell you is this," Captain Hank quietly spoke, "The old protectors, kings, and queens never 'needed' to marry, but if you do – the moment you marry and have all the treasures in your possession – piracy will cease to exist on the island and surrounding seas." Captain Hank concluded.

Teddy added an additional piece of information, "If you are going to marry – it will have to be in two days on the day you turn eighteen. Unless a pirate marries into the family first." Teddy nervously shifted his gaze between August and Helena.

Helena and August had not been privy to a calendar for so long they did not realize the countdown Lexus stated was their own eighteenth birthdays.

CHAPTER 22

Helena picked up a stick from the ground, slightly tapping August with the branch. He pushed it lightly away as she repeated her action.

"Stop," he said forcefully holding her arm. She saw fear in his eyes, not anger towards her, and she trusted him. He was looking behind her and then around them. "What just happened?" He asked her. She was afraid to look, but turned herself around with her back against him tightly, as she looked at what August saw.

They were in a large throne room, surrounded by many thrones. The seats were set in pairs of two, and in the seats were couples. The couples wore veils, full armor, and robes. People walked forward from behind the thrones. "Who are you…" Helena began to ask. August was clinging to Helena to protect her.

A cheerful woman with a sheer veil came forward, taking Helena's hand. The man she left in his seat, who was beside her, spoke from where he was, in a less than cheerful tone in their minds, *"We are the 'Lences and Graces' of the past - preserved."* They were the ancient ones from before the royals.

August Bridges was once again gripping Helena's hand in his own. *"I thought you were dead*?" August asked fearfully, *"How are any of you still alive?"* He demanded.

The woman answered, "How can you die when you never have the ability to be sick or hurt? We are dead, our bodies are not. Our conscious minds transcend from beyond, and our bodies drink healing springs every day." Above them was the water and beneath them was the gems from the cave no man could mine.

Helena reached forward, swirling her hands in the water. It was thick in front of them, yet nothing kept it from consuming the space below.

"In this space we address each other by our full names," The woman spoke, *"So, young ones, what are your full names?"*

"Augustine Thadius Lence Bridges," August answered with a blush.

"That's handsome, by the way," Helena whispered close to his cheek. It was her turn now. "Helena G. Hank," she presented herself. She could not bring herself to share her middle name.

The woman said, "Augustine Thadius, you are a very good leader, and Helena G Hank, you are very good at pressing your luck. You two have a chance to end this plague of curses. You may never find a human on this earth that will use those treasures correctly. You can see each other's minds better now than we could on our last days. You have unity without the treasures, and that makes you the best of us. We trust you with the Talley Gulf Treasures. Bring new life to it. It is in your hands, and you must choose carefully. Not based on us or others, but an informed decision on your own.

If you leave, Helena, it will leave all responsibility on August. There are no guarantees he will succeed. When he comes here. He will be able to speak with you across the world – if you listen. Augustine Thadius Lence Bridges, you must keep the branch with you - to return here. It is from the first tree of the island, and the only way to go to the source. All the treasures are fruits of the tree.

Helena and August nodded their heads. He could feel Helena's burden, and that this woman would take her off the island if he let her go. He held on tighter. Helena realized, this was the branch that Teddy had found. Helena handed it to August, as she felt the burden on his shoulders.

August entered Helena's mind, as she thought to him, "*What if I run away? This is my opportunity...*"

"*I want to marry you one day.*" He answered her, "*I will keep my word, 'if you can leave – I will do my best while you are gone.*" August took her face in his hand and thought, "*Your freedom isn't something I can give to you. You must choose to take it, and if you do, I will keep the pirates at bay myself in your absence.*" He kissed her forehead. Helena did not give him an answer, and he did not think any words. He knew her choice as he looked into her eyes.

The other Lences and Graces did as well, as they too, could hear their thoughts as conversation. The last of the Lences stood up, and he handed August a sword and a coat. These were things that his ancestors held, but they were not bulky or old fashioned, but timeless and fitting. It did not look like he changed much at all. "*This sword is not for blood,*" the Lence stated. August did not understand, but he knew he would be returning to the spiritual throne room often to learn, but more importantly to talk to Helena.

Sunshine peeked through the water in the cave, as they watched the view before embarking on their last efforts to seal their own fates. Helena put her hand over August's hand, which rested on the hilt of the sword.

Chapter 23

Only August returned to where they were before. When Augustine returned without Helena, again, Captain Hank was furious, and left the island shortly after. He reunited with Madison and was surprised to reunite with his daughter in England. He saw them both as often as he could.

August became the Lence without a Grace on his eighteenth birthday. He tried with no avail to find his sister, and his parents. The prophecy was enacted in a way that no one anticipated, as Mark did steal Avril away. This left August to fight with the pirates every night, and rest during the day. He never let the branch out of his hand, and used it as what most islanders assumed was a cane.

August forged an alliance with Lexus, Teddy, and the Pages. He understood that they were allies despite their trying personalities. He grew weary and tired, but the treasures kept him strong and clear.

He would go often to the 'Collective,' which was what he called the throne room of the Lences and the Graces. At first, August and Helena talked every day using their abilities, but as their trials in life increased their connection lessened. He wondered what would have happened if Helena Hank had stayed. There would be less bloodshed, less death, and less loss of great things. He managed to do what he promised he would do, and he kept them at bay to the best of his ability.

He rediscovered the castle ruins, cobb-webs surrounded what was left of the chairs, tables, and furniture. He climbed lose bricks and rocks to enter the remaining tower. It had been untouched by the fire. This tower was where he started on rebuilding the government.

The days had passed with certain adventures and the known Talley Gulf treasures were gathered again in the castle, protected by the Lence, Augustine. The people grew stronger under his leadership as the years passed. Children had grown up and lessons were learned. Fears were overcome and danger escaped. People that needed protection were being protected. Many lives were changed forever.

August would plan his wedding to Helena for the day she would return. He pictured it as the brightest and clearest blue-sky day, with the puffiest white clouds covering the overpowering sunlight. Everyone would wear white clothes and yellow gold jewelry. Helena and August would have all the treasures present in the newly constructed garden built specifically for the occasion by August and his people. Their vows would be written and rehearsed sincerely to each other, exchanging the reality ring, and expanding glass circle. They would seal their promises with a kiss. There would be a flash of lightning as they married, and the people would take it as a sign.

He waited for her every night. However, in the silence of the Collective, he would hear the pirates marching. He would draw his sword, the main Talley Gulf Treasure, and step outside of his castle. He would stab the Lence sword into the sand of the beach; the sand would become the same dust as the coins he once used to fight. The pirates could not step on the sand when he did this, but he knew they were out there, even if they were now few.

August Bridges waited for Helena Hank to return for thirteen years, as Helena Hank became a great surgeon. When Helena returned, she found a ruggedly handsome hero, who fell in love with her again. His traumas were unhealed, but he dealt extensively with them as a prerequisite for their marriage.

Helena began a journey of healing those who lived on the island. After months of establishing herself as a respected healer, a group of pirates stood outside her place of operations. While she helped a pirate man who had lost his leg, she noticed a woman with them who wore a fine, face covering. The woman was adorned in jewelry, and had beautiful grey eyes. Helena realized very quickly that this woman was Avril. Helena was correct in her assumption, and August was reunited with his sister and Helena with her dear friend.

Soon after, the island had reinstated the monarchy due to August's leadership. He was King Augustine the Lence and she became Dr. Helena Hank the Grace, and together they rid the island of pirates to protect the Talley Gulf Treasure.

The End.

Acknowledgments

Special Thanks to

    Andrea Williams

    Carol L. Crymble

    Jonathan Watson

    Rachel Boyer

    Olivia Bowman

    Anna McCarthy

About the Author

My name is Andrea Hope Stanzione. I am from Asheville, North Carolina. While I am not a pirate, I do occasionally write about them. My interests vary from painting and working in an optical office, to writing manuscripts, and video editing. I received my Bachelor's Degree in Cinema/Television. Writing stories has always been a part of my life.